AMERICAN ABSURD

AMERICAN ABSURD

A Work *of* Fiction

Pierre Schlag

Bowen Press

GRAND RAPIDS, MICHIGAN

Published 2016 by Bowen Press
A project of The Dunbar Group, LLC
Grand Rapids, Michigan 49506
http://www.BowenPressBooks.com

ISBN 978-0-692-62144-8

Cataloging-in-Publication data is available from the Library of Congress.

Printed in the United States of America

For Elisabeth

Aperçus

It happened on Santa Monica Boulevard just east of the Avenue of the Stars in Century City. The Black Mercedes E Series 350 coughed. It choked and heaved, and then it died. In the left-hand lane. Mercifully, it was not rush hour. Still, it was embarrassing. The Triple A truck driver spoke with authority. "You're out of gas," he said.

David had no idea how he could have forgotten to fill the tank. This had never happened before. Sure, several times it had been close. But not that close. The Mercedes E Series was conservative in regard to gasoline reserves and warning lights. It's one of the mid-important reasons David chose the Mercedes.

David was annoyed. This seemed appropriate given what David had just learned from the Triple A guy. David's E series, the 350 4MATIC, was an all-wheel-drive vehicle. (This much David knew.) What he didn't know and had just learned was that an all-wheel drive vehicle cannot be towed except with a platform truck. As for getting a platform truck, he had just been informed that it would take at least another hour and a half (by which point, of course, it would be rush hour).

This unwelcome bit of news was more than enough to justify annoyance. But the real story here is that David had a pressing need to pee. And amidst the mass of urban glass and concrete, it was not clear at all to David where or how this could be done. He looked up at the dark glass towers of Century City and decided that things did not look promising. *When did architecture become so inhuman?* he wondered. *Why so large-scale? And why no restroom on the first floor?* (He surmised there would be none.) These questions had never occurred to David before, and he found himself without answers. His bladder, however, was not in the least interested in this or any other tangent. It couldn't wait much longer. Thinking was no doubt a fine thing. But the time for that was past. Action—that was the thing needed now.

David was thus forced to consider what every American male has, at one time or another, been forced to consider—namely, the universal question of whether to hold out and face the unavoidable risks or simply to boldly take things into one's own hands and pee in the street like a man. Looking around, David experienced acute anxiety as he realized that no matter which way he faced, he would remain in full view of the traffic or the buildings—or worse, the traffic *and* the buildings. David tried to recall which of the five dark towers housed his law firm, Green, Friedman & Balsam. Again his bladder showed no interest.

For David, the universal question had long ceased to be hypothetical. He tried to remember how he had answered the question on earlier occasions (surely this must have happened before?) but nothing came to mind. Forced to confront the issue anew, he decided that the risk was simply not worth it. And so the default would go to the other side.

Soon.

The truck driver meanwhile asked David for his Triple A number. David found his card and rattled off the numbers. "5574220917840974." The tow truck driver read them back. "5574220917840934."

"No that's a seven four."

The truck driver scratched his bald pate. David's bladder intimated it might secede and go it alone.

"That's what I got. Can I read it back?"

David was now squeezing hard with his left hand. "No. Can we do this later?"

The truck driver nodded and walked slowly back to his truck. David stepped up to the curb. He ripped open his zipper, dug deeply into his blue boxers, and pulled up with one swift move. Nothing happened. But then, miracle of miracles, a powerful, translucent stream issued forth, spraying in a perfect and magnificent arc onto the asphalt of Santa Monica Boulevard. David had never felt such relief. He looked around to see if anyone was watching. Not with fear or dread, as previously imagined, but instead proudly—as if the passersby would inexorably have to acknowledge (and approve) the geometric acuity and undeniable manliness of the spectacle before them.

To David's chagrin, no one was watching save a middle-aged blonde driving a white Lexus who whipped her head around in obvious shock as she sped past in the left lane.

Settling into grateful appreciation and contemplating the steady calm of his diminishing stream, David placed his left hand on his hips and leaned slightly forward on the balls of his feet. *Well done*, he thought. He could not believe that he ever worried about this. The universal question was not only answered, but decisively so. David tried to recall whether he had ever peed with such authority.

It was at this point that he felt a hand on his shoulder and turned around to see a man in a dark uniform wearing the unmistakable cap of the Los Angeles Police Department.

[DRAFT PROOFS]

The New Amsterdam Magazine
Title: "L.A. Unsustainable"
Byline: J.T.
Publication Date: ______
Dep't. of Cultural Affairs

"L.A. Unsustainable"

By J.T.

L.A. conjures up images of smog. But in early October, there are these crisp, sunny, wind-blown days when L.A. shines in all its glory. Today, the sky is a crystalline blue with puff-white clouds. The palms sway gently in the breeze. It is as if the earth itself exults with exuberance and fecundity. On Sunset Boulevard, the glossy-coated cars race to the beach or Beverly Hills or wherever. The gears shift. The engines purr. The chrome sparkles and gleams.

One of these cars is a BMW 5 Series. Alone at the wheel is a person—let's say a hypothetical person. By occupation, he is probably a lawyer, a contractor, or a businessman. Possibly a consultant of some sort. He is on average 45, married, has 2.1 children, has had 3.2 affairs, and very likely owns a deeply mortgaged Spanish stucco house in Brentwood, Westwood, or maybe Bel Air. People think he might be connected to the entertainment industry—an impression he does little to discourage.

He is greatly overworked, though in truth, he never actually does any work. He might have an office—often he thinks so—but if he does, he never actually gets there and, in fact, has no idea where it is located. Still, every morning he leaves the house at 7:25. Invariably, he spends the day driving from place to place—Century City to the beach, Downtown to Hollywood, Santa Monica to Studio City. Sometimes there are appointments or meetings—doctor's visits, meetings with contractors, shopping. But most of the time, there aren't—it's a question of simply going from one place to another. It's become so much a part of his daily routine that he has stopped wondering why things happen this way. In fact, it's doubtful he ever wondered. In any event, it's the way things are.

Or at least that's how he understands it. If you ask this person what the point is, he will tell you: the point is to get from point A to point B. That is his essential function: to get from A to B. If you ask what happens next, the answer is that whenever point B is reached, it becomes a new point A relative to some new point B. And so on and so forth.

Some people believe that there are a great many like him. And not just on the West Side, but in Pasadena and San Marino. In Orange County. The exact number remains unknown, but it is not small. Many of them drive a Mercedes—the car of choice in L.A. Others have BMWs, Lexuses, Infinitis, Audis, and more recently, the Porsche Panamera. Most of the drivers are men. The women, however, are just as capable—and in fact widely believed to be more reliable. They are either 47 or 35. (The other stats are similar.) And, of course, they never make it to the office either. They simply drive from point A to point B.

In 2005, Tony White, a doctoral anthropology student at U.C. Berkeley and founding member of a commune on an artichoke farm in the Russian River valley, produced a critical dissertation on the subject. Tony is a thin, scruffy-looking man with a wispy brown beard and dark, glowing eyes. He favors large Americanos and smells of cigarettes, though I have never seen him smoke. The first time I presented him with my press credentials, he balked. "What could a *New Amsterdam* writer want with an unemployed post-grad?" he asked. Two weeks later, we were sitting at a coffee house near Telegraph and Durant in Berkeley.

When I brought up the dissertation, he flinched.

"You know, it was never published. And they almost didn't pass me."

"Why?"

"Politics. They thought it was too political." A faint smirk passed his lips.

"I take it you didn't think it was political?"

"Oh no, it was political all right. I just didn't think it would matter that much."

Tony then explained that it was not so much the empirical research on the L.A. drivers (the multiple regression analyses) nor the interviews (there were only 24, and some were ambiguous) nor even his intimations of questionable connections to City Hall. All that was "totally par for the course—totally expected of a cultural studies project," he said. The real objection was, and he mouthed the phrase with obvious distaste, "the irrationalist strain of my thesis. Look," he said, "the more I studied the thing, the more puzzling it became. At some point, I started questioning the entire enterprise."

"When?"

"It was gradual. But if there's a single moment that stands out, it was an evening at the Trix Bar and Grill. It's on College. My girlfriend and I and another couple. I explained it to them."

The explanation Tony gave me was quite convoluted. Tony White thinks dialectically—positing an idea and then offering a counter. He started by explaining what he called "the deep structure" of the thing. The idea, as Tony recounted, of getting from point A to point B could be understood in any number of ways. There was Lakoff and Johnson's source-path-goal schema—the root metaphor that underlies so many human activities—law, business, politics, literature. There were all the eschatologies—Christian, Hegelian, Marxian. There was the psychology of growth stages—Piaget, Maslow, Kohlberg, Gilligan. In microeconomics, there was maximization.

"So pretty much everything we've been told is about going from point A to point B," he said with growing excitement. "To think otherwise, for most people, seems like complete nonsense. As for L.A.—it simply adapted the thing to local circumstances. Look, it's L.A. If the point is to get from A to B, then it's no surprise that in L.A. a big part of it would be done by car. People more or less eased into it."

"But . . ." Here Tony stopped and looked into my eyes. I sensed the counter-story coming. "But . . . that doesn't answer the fundamental question, does it? Why? Why do this? When I started my interviews, I hit a brick wall. I'd ask the drivers why, and the response was always the same. 'It's what we do,' they said. 'But why do you do it?' 'It's who we are,' they said."

"But how to do they support themselves?"

"Some are rich. Others ultimately go back to work at some point. But even then they relapse. They go back to driving from A to B. It's fascinating to watch. They actually believe, at least while they're doing it, that this is the point of life. That this is what they're supposed to be doing. And denial always helps—you know, it fills in the gaps. Some of them absolutely refuse to talk about it."

"So what happened with the dissertation?"

"When it came to my thesis defense—you know, the oral part of the dissertation—I really pushed it, and it was obvious the committee was really upset. I told them, "This going from A to B, this source-path-goal, this eschatological drive, this maximization thing, this growth thing—it isn't going anywhere." Tony glanced up at me to see if I was following. "It's treadmill ontology," he added unhelpfully. He could see I was skeptical. "Think of it this way," he said. "We are constantly—that's the key word here, constantly—going from A to B. People register the A-to-B part. But they always fail to notice the 'constantly.' 'Constantly going from A to B—get it?' The dynamism is encased in the stasis! It's a constant!"

To get a different perspective, I talked to Scott Daubert, a young and surprisingly intellectual Chamber of Commerce representative—one of the New Conservatives. Mr. Daubert is lithe, genial, and seemingly interested in everything. He admits to liking workouts in the gym and long runs on Huntington Beach. In a throwback to a prior generation, he drinks Perrier only—ice, but no lime. I asked him about Tony White's dissertation. He sighed and gestured to brush lint from his freshly pressed pant leg. "It's déjà vu, old news," he said. "Everyone who's anyone has known about this for a long time. Frankly, I don't think there is anything to be made of it. All these drivers are among those who help make L.A. be L.A. They are social constructionists," he said, smiling with the self-assurance of the au courant. "And what they construct, or more accurately, help construct, is L.A. Getting from point A to point B in shiny, new luxury cars—that's a lot of what we do in L.A." He smiles. "I can tell you the COC is one hundred percent behind this—at least the L.A. Chapter."

I asked him about why the women were always 47 and 35. "We noticed that," he said. "The COC looked into it sometime ago. I don't really know what came of it. We may have issued a report. I'll send it to you if there is one."

"Mr. White has argued that the whole thing—the going from A to B—is pointless or very nearly pointless," I pressed.

"Yes, well, dissertations have to be written. But you don't see the COC writing up reports on the value of dissertations." I pressed him again. Mr. Daubert explained that ever since the publication of "Apology and Critique," it's been "baseline" that the only way criticism gets going is by perversely presuming that the purpose of a thing is to be other than what it is. "The liberal-left has been running that gambit for decades. But without that—criticism can't get off the ground. These people are driving from A to B—that's what they do." He folded his hands. I could sense a certain self-satisfaction.

I pointed out that the purpose of driving from A to B seems to be to get somewhere, but that the drivers in question don't really get anywhere. Every B just becomes another A for yet another B. He smiled and pointed out that, in terms of rational choice theory, it's really up to the individual drivers to decide on the value of their activity. "You know, the COC really does believe in the free market. For us, it's not simply a convenient position."

When he served as Tony White's thesis adviser, Dr. Max Stein was a professor at the University of California Berkeley. Today, he is the Charles M. Fairmont Chair in Cognitive and Rhetorical Studies. When I caught up with him in his office at Berkeley and asked about Tony White, Professor Stein immediately responded, "A brilliant young man." And then speaking more slowly, he added, "But Tony was always a bit headstrong. It was apparent from the first. The key thing about a dissertation thesis (and this is true at any school) is that it be plausible and ably documented. Tony had problems with both aspects. He had this critical obsession with instrumentalism—the 'A-to-B thing' as he called it. Ultimately, it blindsided him."

"How?"

"He came to celebrate, even worship, purposeless activities. These would be activities not structured as going from A to B. Anyway it was a complete non-starter," Dr. Stein explained. "You see, psychologists have tried to study the question of whether or not purposeless activities such as—oh I don't know, say, wandering—contribute to happiness or well-being. It's a very difficult problem. The thing is, we cannot isolate a fundamentally purposeless activity—one that does not involve getting from A to B. The whole question brings considerable philosophical complexities into play."

"Like what?"

"Well, is it the case that there are in fact no purposeless activities, or do we, the investigators, suffer from a variant of the Observer's Paradox—such that any time we isolate an activity, we perforce find some purpose in it? I am afraid we just don't know the answer. Are we hardwired in this way? Is it language? Culture? We just don't know. The research is arrested," he says, a mix of chagrin and bemusement on his face. Asked about recent empirical studies at Northwestern on the subject, he drew back. "Substandard. For now, the smart money is on Cornell. But we're going to have to wait."

I saw Tony White a couple months later at a summer solstice celebration near the Russian River, north of San Francisco. As we sipped the remains of a local Syrah on the patio of a very weathered ranch house, I shared Scott Daubert's and Dr. Stein's thoughts.

"You talked to the Chamber of Commerce?" Tony asked in surprise.

"Yes."

"Why? I'm sorry, but if it's the Chamber of Commerce, I have strictly no comment. Do you have *any idea* who those people *are*?" (In all our interviews, this was the only time Tony raised his voice.)

I deflected. "Let's talk about Dr. Stein—what do you make of his suggestion that you are a partisan of purposeless activities?"

Tony's answer was clipped: "First, in my entire dissertation, I never once used the expression 'purposeless activity.' That's a complete distortion of my work. Plus it would be truly nutty. Second, you know what Max Stein said to me after the oral defense? He took me in his office, closed the door, and said, 'Tony, you have to make peace with it. The point is to get from A to B. There is nothing else. Destroy that and people will have nothing—nothing at all.' Now, tell me: that's not politics?" Tony asked, finishing his wine in a single swallow.

The Breakdown

Public urination is a relatively rare infraction on the Century City beat, and so the LAPD officer had to call in to get the ordinance number. David appreciated the man's professionalism and politeness—everything but the way the man had clasped David's shoulder from behind. To David, that had seemed a touch too personal.

David could not believe his bad luck. Why did this have to happen to him? First, the car ran out of gas. Then, the infraction. David's affects now came automatically, one by one: anger, shame, embarrassment, and then all of them together—an unstable mélange of emotional toxicity.

"Sir, where were you going?"

"To Hollywood."

"You, uh . . . live there?"

"No. I was—" David tried to think why he was driving to

Hollywood, but he could not recall. Nothing came to mind. This morning he had driven to Santa Monica, then to Venice, back through Culver City, and now he was on his way to Hollywood. Surely, there had to be some good reason. It's just that David could not remember what it was.

But why should he, really? Must there be a reason? Wasn't the driving enough—the fact that he was driving somewhere, going from here to there? There was pleasure in it. And a certain freedom. David particularly enjoyed driving the Mercedes after it had just been washed. The car itself was pristine—a solid black clear coat, the automotive equivalent of formal wear. The suspension was pleasantly supple. The engine, smooth. The leather still smelled new. And he could go anywhere. Anywhere at all. He was, of course, always going from here to there, but once he arrived, there became another here to yet another there (and so on and so forth). There was always somewhere to drive. Plus, he could choose the order of the here and there. As well as the routes. And, barring traffic, he could choose the speed. His lane changes could vary—ranging from the abrupt and aggressive to the genial and accommodating. On occasion, some lane changes were even impromptu—as when he wasn't paying attention.

Plus there was a sense of community. Mercedes, BMW, Lexus, Infiniti, Audi—they were part of the same family. There was a sense of well-being that suffused David's entire being when he looked around him and saw drivers contentedly driving these new, gleaming, upscale cars. They were part of the same enterprise, the same lifestyle. They manifestly took pleasure in each other's pleasure. David certainly did, and he was fairly sure the other drivers did as well. He could look left as he was waiting in his lane for the light to change, see a BMW 5 Series, and think, *That driver could be me. And I could be him. We are cut of the same cloth. We appreciate the same things. And most of all, we appreciate driving around L.A. on these amazing sunny days.* David felt that the sense of community was very strong on the West Side—particularly the northern part of the West Side. Which is why he generally favored driving in those areas: Brentwood, Westwood, Santa Monica, and Pacific Palisades. And, of course, Beverly Hills.

Then too, part of the appeal was the challenge. Yesterday, for instance, leaving the gates of his subdivision, he was faced right away with a broadcast on KFOB that announced a SigAlert on the 405. Construction blocked Wilshire. Santa Monica at Sepulveda was a mess. Ohio was out of the question. He made a command decision to head north to Sunset and then take a right. The move had been a success. The outflanking maneuver had bypassed the obstructions. Sunset was wide open—only a few cars here and there. David had planned to go to the office. He could not recall precisely where his office was located. But no matter. He had driven from here to there and, all in all, yesterday had been a success. True—he never did make it to the office, but that was to be expected. It had been a good day. Today was not.

"So should I still take the car?" the Triple A guy asked.

"Of course you should take the car!"

"Sir, you don't need to shout," said the police officer. "This is a minor offense. Let's just keep it that way, shall we?"

"Keep it what way?"

"Sir, this will just take a few more moments. Why don't you just sit here on the curb."

David repeated the words: "Sit here on the curb! *Sit here* on the curb! Who does this guy think he is?"

"I don't need to sit," said David.

"Sir, I'm going to have to ask you to comply."

David put both hands on his hips and gave a sharp laugh.

The police officer sighed and put his ticket book away. "Sir, I'm going to have to ask you to put your hands on the trunk, legs spread wide."

"What?"

David's surprise was to no avail. The police officer repeated his instruction, hooked David's triceps from behind, and pushed him gently but firmly to the trunk of the police cruiser.

"Officer, there's a misunderstanding. I didn't mean—"

"Sir, please stand still. You have the right to remain silent. You have the right . . ."

■ ■ ■

On the twelfth floor of 1500 Avenue of the Stars, John Morrison of Sterling & Packard, Attorneys at Law, was bored. He had been looking out his window, watching the traffic go by for the last ten or fifteen minutes. As he well knew, having done this many times before, there was nothing to be seen out there. Absolutely nothing except the traffic going by, coming to a stop at the red lights, and then proceeding forward again. The cars took lefts or rights, or they went straight through. It was the essence of nothingness happening. And yet looking down onto this nothingness seemed to John Morrison vastly superior to working on the Aronson deal (which had barely inched forward ever since it arrived on his desk nearly ten months ago).

It's easy to imagine, then, John Morrison's surprise and emergent gratitude when, looking down, he saw LAPD police cruiser 127 (the number was on the roof), lights flashing red and blue, right behind a slick black Mercedes. The police officer was apparently cuffing a well-dressed, middle-aged man. This just did not happen on Santa Monica Boulevard in Century City. Farther east? Yes, definitely. Farther west? On occasion. But on Santa Monica Boulevard at Avenue of the Stars? Not in this lifetime. And cuffing a man in a brand new black Mercedes—an E Series? Never.

This sudden and unforeseen interruption of John Morrison's long-suffering, soul-sapping ennui propelled him to do something completely out of character—namely, to race to the elevator and rush down to investigate.

"Officer, why are you arresting this man?"

"Sir, please step back."

"Actually, I am a lawyer."

"Well, good for you," said the officer.

"Thank God," said David. "He's arresting me because I ran out of gas and I had to relieve myself."

"Officer, I'm sure there is a good explanation for this."

"Step back, sir." The officer leaned his head down to access his microphone. "A-127—need backup. We have a 148, Code 2 at Santa Monica Boulevard and Avenue of the Stars."

"Now, look here, there's no call for that," said John.

"Will you help me?" asked David.

"You mean represent you? No. Absolutely not. Well, maybe."

David felt his luck turning.

"Don't say another word," said John. "Officer, why are you arresting my client?"

"Your client, now? Okay. We'll play it your way. Public urination and indecent exposure. I haven't done it yet, but if you want, I could add resisting arrest. Would you like me to do that?" The police officer was unfailingly polite. Punctilious.

"What's he talking about?" John asked David.

"He wanted me to sit on the curb, and I said no."

"Don't say another word."

The backup police cruiser pulled up. That made two black and whites behind a black Mercedes. So now it was two police officers consulting and two men in suits sitting cuffed on the curb. (John Morrison somehow crossed the line from legal representation to obstructing a law enforcement officer and was invited to join David on the curb.) A small crowd was watching. And it was all happening at the intersection of Santa Monica Boulevard and Avenue of the Stars. At rush hour. Traffic was backing up all the way to Westwood Boulevard.

■ ■ ■

Two floors above John Morrison's law firm was Incandescence, Inc. There, Mariana Fleischman, literary agent and media representative, was also looking down at the scene. Critically. Professionally. A Stanford graduate in cognitive science, Mariana, now 42 (35 to her friends, ageless to everyone else), had arrived. Really arrived. She was way beyond doing mere agent's work. She was a publicist. She made media stars happen. Her conceit was that she could make a star out of anyone—anyone at all. Not because they were star material, but because she was Mariana.

And so when she noticed the Black Mercedes together with the two handcuffed middle-aged men in suits sitting on the curb and the two police cruisers, she saw a challenge. She pulled out a cheap, disposable cell phone from her purse, used for just this kind of occasion, and called 911.

"There's an incident at Santa Monica and Avenue of the Stars."

"OK, ma'am, please tell me your location and your name."

"There's an incident—oh my god, that man has just hit a police officer! Oh, my god, I have to go." For Mariana, lying came easy.

Then she called KZLA 9News. "There's an incident at Santa Monica and Avenue of the Stars. They've hit a police officer. It looks like the beginning of a riot. You'll need a helicopter."

She threw the disposable cell phone in the wastebasket and called in her assistant. "Trish, what kind of car do you drive?"

"A Mazda Miata."

"What year?"

"I got it new four years ago."

"Can you loan it to me?"

"What's wrong with your Lexus?"

"Nothing. I just lent it to a friend. I need a car right away."

Mariana held out her hands for the keys. Trish reached into her purse and handed them over. Down in the parking garage, Mariana wondered how long it would actually take to round the corner onto Santa Monica Boulevard—what with the traffic and all. With smiles and waves, she wound her way out of the parking structure. It took a full ten minutes at least, but finally she turned right onto Santa Monica. She aimed the Mazda straight for the black Mercedes, pressed lightly on the gas, and delivered a glancing blow to the driver's side door. Perfect.

The Confrontation

David Madden had not seen J.T.'s "L.A. Unsustainable" article. He didn't subscribe to *The New Amsterdam*. It was not his sort of magazine. Moreover, the article had not been published yet. But if David had read the article (which he couldn't have), he likely would have recognized himself as one of the L.A. drivers—the sort of person who drives in his new luxury car from A to B repeatedly, pretty much throughout the day.

And if he had read the article, he probably would have agreed with the Chamber of Commerce guy. So people were driving around? Big deal. That's what people did in L.A. And if some, like himself, did it more than others, well, so what?

The so what, of course, is that not all of these drivers ended up inexplicably failing to put gas in the car, stalling on Santa Monica Boulevard, creating epic traffic jams, forgetting where they were going, and being arrested for public urination. That was different.

David had put off telling Eloise about the Century City fiasco last night, but this morning there was no way around it. Sitting at the lustrous black and pink granite island in his kitchen, protectively hunched over his almond granola with 1 percent yogurt, David waited patiently for Eloise to come down for breakfast. He would certainly have to tell her about running out of gas and how this crazy woman deliberately crashed into him at Century City. And he would have to tell her about the ticket and the court date. The police officer had released him on his own recognizance. While that was certainly better than going off to jail, the experience was still a bit raw. It's not every day that one ends up handcuffed, sitting on the curb of Santa Monica Boulevard.

Plus there had been the resulting traffic jam—a monster line of stopped cars choking Santa Monica Boulevard all the way back to the San Diego Freeway. It had made the local news. There was even a KZLA 9News video of David handcuffed, sitting on the curb next to his ersatz lawyer, John Morrison.

He would tell Eloise as soon as she came down.

As it turned out, things took a very different turn that morning. Eloise poured herself coffee. She sat brusquely opposite David. Her porcelain cup clanked against the granite counter.

"Chlamydia," she said.

"Chlamydia?" asked David, looking up, baffled.

He couldn't grasp what this had to do with anything or why Eloise was saying the name so emphatically. It was a lyrical name, he thought. From Greek mythology, probably: Electra, Cassandra—Chlamydia. It would have been a great name for their daughter—certainly more distinctive than Emily.

But Eloise had insisted on Emily. And back when Emily was born, no one suggested Chlamydia. David had never heard the name until this moment in fact.

"Chlamydia," Eloise said once again. More emphatically. David wondered what sort of response was appropriate to this one-word declaration, but nothing came to mind. Perhaps a great aunt had died?

"David! It's an STD."

This was truly confusing. Was Eloise telling him that she had contracted an STD? Why? When? And why was he called upon to deal with STDs so early in the morning, when he had yet to finish his first cup of coffee? It seemed unfair somehow.

And then, from some forgotten recess of the deep mind, came an image both sharply focused and undeniable.

"Oh," he said.

"How old is she?"

"I don't know."

"You don't know???? She doesn't have birthdays?"

This was confusing. Why was Eloise jumping all over the place like this? *She doesn't have birthdays?*—what kind of question was that?

"How *old* is she, David?"

"Honey, it was just once. It was so long ago. I am so sorry. Incredibly sorry. It was an accident."

"Accident? Really? I don't think so."

But it had been an accident, or at least as close to an accident as such things can be, which, as David thought about it, is not all that much. Okay—so it wasn't an accident. It was at his twentieth high school reunion—an event fraught with risk. There were the old flames. The old flames who never were. Those who never were, but might have been. Those who should have been. And those who damned well could be now (regardless of what they were back then). All of these possibilities made the high school reunion a dangerous social arena.

At the reception, David had negotiated these risks (which, in his case, remained somewhat hypothetical in any event) with aplomb. It was a waitress who did him in. And not at the party, but afterwards. She found him in the hotel hallway outside the Lincoln Convention Ballroom sitting alone after the ceremony. He was tipsy, so she had taken him home. Her home.

David wanted to apologize again, to explain. But all explanations were clichéd, all apologies gratuitous. And once spoken, none sounded good enough. Because, as David realized in that moment, they weren't.

"Damn you," Eloise said, spinning around and marching off down the long corridor towards the canary yellow bathroom at the other end of the house. David heard the bathroom door slam.

This was not a good sign.

Not at all. In David's experience, this was at once ominous and ambivalent. Over the years he had learned that, for Eloise, the bathroom was a nearly magical space. It wasn't something that he could conceptualize or articulate very well, but intuitively, he had learned the relevant operative principles. In retreat mode, the bathroom provided his wife a safe haven to cry in peace and console herself. In offensive mode, it was the tactical space of withdrawal used for the replenishment of energy, the marshaling of resources, and the fortification of arguments—all in preparation for a world-class fight. In short, it was a room of utter and unspeakable treachery.

And it certainly didn't help any that the retreat and the offensive modes called for diametrically opposed responses. In retreat mode, Eloise was best left alone. Even a mild knock on the door, accompanied by gentle entreaties to come out, could provoke a radical and disastrous change in attitude—from quiet resignation to murderous rage. In offensive mode, by contrast, the important thing was to interrupt (no matter what the cost) the planning and strategizing going on in there. In this circumstance, the essential thing was to engage in dialogue of whatever kind—no matter how strained, incoherent, or punishing it might be.

The great problem, of course, as David had learned over the years, lay in knowing which was which. And since the door was always closed (opening it was tantamount to the nuclear option), there was absolutely no way of knowing.

To say that David was thinking all these things at this particular time would be a lie. But over fourteen years of marriage, he had intuited his way there. David was not an intellectual by any means. But he was not insensitive, and he was not dumb. He knew.

And thus it was that he skulked out of the house while Eloise was still in the bathroom. It wasn't merely cowardice (although that was certainly part of it) but also the best thing to do at that time for all concerned. Or so he told himself. That, plus he had to get to the office.

■ ■ ■

On the way to the office (except not), David felt a new and unpleasant sensation slowly seeping into the little corners of his being like a low-level toxic spill. It was guilt, and it would not be contained. He tried some arguments. In his favor, it could be said that the affair had happened more than three years ago. Moreover (now, there's a word!), it really couldn't count as an affair at all—more like a one-night stand. And when one thought about it, barely that, really. More like a bump in the night. Admittedly, a repetitive erotic kind of bump, of course, but . . . And there was the problem once again. All in all, there was no way around it: He had screwed up. How could this have happened?

As he looked down the eight lanes of Wilshire Boulevard, David forgot the waitress and recalled his first encounter with Eloise. He had just turned twenty-eight that spring. It was a spring like any other, except that this spring, David found himself subject to the sudden and apparently non-negotiable demands of his cultural code. He was virtually commanded, as if by some previously unnoticed higher power, to go out and seek a mate. David was, in this regard (the focused drive to find a mate), a late bloomer, but this tardiness produced a certain intensity and concentration that might otherwise have been lacking.

And so it was that at the age of twenty-eight, David launched a systematic search for the essence of womanhood. He started off with fern bars—places he deemed to be among the most auspicious venues. As David saw the matter, if the essence of womanhood could be found at all, surely a fern bar would be the place. The fact that fern bars had been seriously out of style for well more than a decade in L.A. (and everywhere else for that matter) is something that completely passed David by. In truth, however, David's radical misreading of cultural mores served as a providential winnowing of his available options. Indeed, when David started his quest, there were only six fern bars left in L.A.—three on the West Side, two in Hollywood, and one in Van Nuys. All of them self-consciously retro. It was at one of these that David met Eloise.

At first David's attention gravitated towards the Van Nuys bar, which carried the promising name "The Green Connection," suggesting an organic wholesomeness bordering on innocence while nonetheless promising connection. Soon, however, David deemed the Van Nuys Bar too seedy, too gaudy, and too loud. And like all fern bars since the beginning of time, it was air conditioned to the hilt. It also had not helped much that on his third or fourth visit to the Green Connection, one of the patrons had stumbled next to David, sending an entire array of happy-hour food flying—a colorful mélange of crab caesar salad, *chili con queso* with red sauce and green flecks, and those little pork sausages so popular long ago—all of it soaked with various multicolor drinks (Campari and soda mostly). David took this as a negative omen. Henceforth, his quest for the essence of womanhood would bypass the Valley entirely. This was just as well because, for some time now, David had started to think that the Valley was pretty much a detour—no matter where you were going.

It took David many outings at the fern bars. But finally he spied her sitting by herself at the bar of the Greenery (a West Side bar). After two minutes of indecision, he walked over and asked, "So what do you drive?" It was not the most imaginative pickup line. It took its place with a long series of equally banal, clichéd, and now passé openings like, "What do you do?" or "Do you come here often?" or the truly cringe-inspiring, "Have we met before?"—a line as inviting and subtle as "I would like coitus with you right now."

"A blue Mazda RX-7," she said.

"With moonroof?" he asked hopefully.

"With moonroof." She smiled and flipped her hair back with one jolt of the head. Her eyes opened wide as she searched for David's reaction.

He nodded in approval.

Needless to say, David was already somewhat into driving. He was still a long way from the A-to-B thing. Indeed, there is no doubt he was gainfully employed at the time (and did in fact show up for work).

"Eloise," she said, holding out her hand.

"David. Stick or automatic?"

"Stick. Five-speed."

"Could I have a sip of your wine?" he asked.

They talked about favorite routes. They both agreed that the on-ramp connecting the Santa Monica freeway to the San Diego (going north) was awesome.

"It's like a movie," said David. "You just careen around that banked curve forever."

"I know! Whenever I take it, I wish had gotten a convertible. It would look so cool."

"Sure, but the Mazda RX-7 is so you."

She blushed.

They were excited in each other's presence. Each of them made the other shine a bit brighter. It all felt very much like flirting. At the very least, David enjoyed their banter. And talking with her made him feel attractive. David recognized, of course, that he was tipsy and that, as far as he could tell, she was too.

In fact, she was smashed. Which was one of the reasons she had long forgotten about the parking meter. When David and Eloise emerged from the Greenery in early evening, the sun was still in full force. After squinting their way down the sidewalk, the harsh, non-negotiable consequences of Eloise's memory lapse became starkly evident: The blue Mazda RX-7 had been booted. The vile and predatory thing was wrapped around the right front wheel. It was a classic bright orange job—an NDF Products heavy-duty Immobilizer.

Eloise gasped. She clutched his arm. He hugged her and stroked her hair. It was the least he could do.

Puzzled, he asked, "You don't pay your parking tickets?"

"Never. You?"

David calmed her down, promised her there would be better days, and most importantly tasked himself with the privilege of driving her home. It was a modest walk-up condo on the southern edge of Studio City. With the rush hour, the drive took the better part of an hour and a half. Conveniently, this allowed Eloise to sober up and compose herself. She invited him in.

To say that one thing led to another, as people so often do in these situations, would overstate the continuity of their dance. There were a few false steps—awkward moments when the action seemed to go backward rather than forward. But ultimately, persistence prevailed. He was a generous and thoughtful lover. To David, Eloise seemed pleased. Contented. "We'll have to do this again," she said, pouring herself a glass of milk.

As for David, he was overwhelmed by boundless gratitude. He had chosen her and she had chosen him. There was (though he would never have called it that) a graceful reciprocity to it all. Putting aside, of course, the Immobilizer.

They saw each other the next day at her place. And the next day. And the day after that. She was a history undergrad from NYU, currently working as an assistant, er, consultant, er, something. He was an ahem, associate, ahem, something or other (which impressed Eloise, albeit not endlessly so).

This then had been the beginning of their courtship. As David thought about it waiting for the left arrow on Beverly Glen at Santa Monica, it was probably not the most robust foundation for a marriage.

But in the end, what was really? And it had worked. He loved her, and she loved him. True, fern bars were not particularly selective places and car-bonding was not the most discriminating criterion, but, to say it again, it had worked. Sure, they had been lucky. But who didn't need luck to make things work these days?

David would make things right. He was sure of it.

■ ■ ■

In the canary yellow downstairs bathroom, Eloise was still bent over forward on the commode. *So! It has come to this!* she thought. David was almost certainly lying—"just once," "an accident," "long ago." *Ha!* She tried to imagine this other woman. Was she a younger, slimmer, edgier version of herself? Or was she instead a complement—dark-haired where she was blond, brown-eyed when she was blue? But these were foolish questions. Without knowing who she was, they were impossible to answer.

Eloise dismissed David's denials and excuses. She just knew that the affair was still going on, that David had as good as been caught in the act.

Eloise had been waiting for this to happen. It was more or less inevitable. The stats did not lie. Eloise knew what she was supposed to feel. She knew she was entitled to be angry, to act out, maybe even throw a few things.

If David was still around (which she doubted) she would definitely throw a few things. She thought of the dreadful beige and blue Woodberry's china they inherited from his mother. It would shatter on impact and make a gratifying crash against the wall. She would demand an immediate end to The Affair. She thought about throwing him out. That's always what happens. But how exactly did that work? In the movies and on TV, the men always slink away compliantly into the night. To a friend's couch. Or better yet, to some soulless motel purgatory. At any rate—somewhere uncomfortable and awkward. But what if David refused? What then?

She felt all these things in quick succession. And as she was feeling these things, this heated brew of compounding negativity, she detected, much to her surprise, a tiny surreptitious current of satisfaction. "An affair," she thought. She tried on some variations: "My husband's affair . . ." "When my husband had an affair, . . ." Or best of all, "When I found out about The Affair . . ." Eloise realized that she was saying it out loud.

At this point, she recognized that not only had she been expecting The Affair, but that in some well-hidden subterranean corner of her being, she had actually in some small way wanted it. Among her closest women friends, most had already encountered The Affair. Some of them several times. Generally, Eloise felt fortunate to be exempt. "There, but for the grace of . . ." et cetera. But she had also worried about what her friends would think if David didn't have an affair soon. They might think he lacked imagination, a certain spark. They might think he was a schlemiel, a dolt—and then what would that make her?

Exploring these thoughts, Eloise discovered yet another small dissenting strain—tinier than the first, but undeniably there as well. Whenever The Affair had come up with her friends, Eloise felt silenced. She had no personal advice to give, no emotional reservoir to tap into, no platform from which to dole out sympathy. She had felt left out.

But now that was over. Eloise felt almost—that was a crucial qualification—pleased. The Affair was a stage. And the sooner it began, the sooner they could get over it. There was no virtue in delay. They would process it—process being what their marriage counselor almost always recommended. For anything. The marriage counselor was always saying things like "Marriage is a process." Or, "You have to process these things." Or again: "It's all a big process. You can't lose sight of that."

Eloise was a bit weary of process—especially since she and David had been processing with the same marriage counselor for more than three years now. In fact, Eloise had communicated her doubts to the marriage counselor: "I'm just not sure if we have all that much left to process," she said. "Couldn't we try something else?" The marriage counselor had said it was a good idea and that she would think about it—"process it."

Eloise knew what that meant. But right now, it didn't matter.

Now, there was new input. They had reached a new stage. Eloise flushed the toilet, though that was more habit than anything else. She assumed that David would have left by now. She didn't even bother to check. Instead, she picked up her cell phone on the granite kitchen counter and called her therapist. She noticed a scratch in the finish. She beseeched the assistant to get her an appointment as soon as possible. She leaned down to check for other scratches.

"Yes, I am totally shattered. I don't know where to turn." And then with a pause followed by a deep inhalation, reprised by a pause again, she said breathlessly, "My husband is having an affair."

■ ■ ■

By that afternoon, Eloise had called five of her closest friends. She had confided her distraught state, cursed an entire gender, and wished all its members eternal perdition. She received resonant ratifications of her righteousness. Solidarity was affirmed. Sisterhood was celebrated. Retaliation was advised. Shopping somehow came up.

Listening to all this, she declared she was "through, absolutely through with men" and wondered silently how the reconciliation with David would go. There was, needless to say, a lot to think about.

By the afternoon, well into her third glass of Conundrum (it was the most expensive wine she could find in David's cellar), the little rivulets of satisfaction from that morning had burgeoned and overrun the pain, the sadness, the anger, the distress. The Affair had transformed Eloise into a woman of substance—someone to be reckoned with. It had only been five hours, but already Eloise was an Affair Survivor.

And then a thought: All this attitude would not do. Her personal therapist would never understand. Here was this semi-humiliating event, and Eloise (at least since noon) wasn't humiliated.

Plus, the currents of satisfaction did not conform to her longstanding diagnostic. The therapist could very well decide that they needed to start from scratch. It would be a huge setback. And who knew how long it would take before they could make progress once again.

Eloise would have to rein herself in, suppress her emerging satisfaction, and compose herself into more appropriate affects—pain, sadness, anger, distress. And exactly in that order too. The only thing she had doubts about was whether all four affects could be communicated in succession within a half-hour session.

The therapist's questions would be predictable. "How does it make you feel? What else do you feel? Is it more anger you feel or is it more sadness? What would you like to happen? Do you think your girlfriends will be supportive? How does this make you feel?" (Again.) "What about your family?"

Eloise finished her glass of wine and decided to take a long, hot bath.

Tomorrow, she would go shopping. Revenge shopping.

The Letdown

J.T. mused that her new article, "L.A. Unsustainable," would probably be nominated for the Charles Zucker award. And if it was nominated, she would probably win. Not the least reason being that she knew Charles Zucker intimately. Emotionally. Intellectually. Carnally. And in all the other ways one might know a person.

Charles Zucker had been her former editor at *The New Amsterdam* and her sponsor as she climbed her way up the treacherous ladders of the New York publishing empires. Perhaps more important, he had been her lover in Paris when she spent those two years working for the expatriate American paper, *The Paris Times*. Even back then, J.T. was on the culture beat—the French culture beat. It was a trying assignment. She realized right away that she could not possibly undo the countless misimpressions of her fellow Americans had about the French. It was a constant tussle with futility. And so it was that J.T. committed herself entirely to her love affair, deciding to make eros her canvas. Another sand-castle in the air to be sure, but really, in the end, weren't they all? J.T. was enough of an existentialist to realize that between politics, journalism, and sex, it was all a choice and just as meaningless one way as another. But she was also enough of a romantic, even this late, to believe that passion could be more than just a movie. As for her native irresponsibility, she dedicated that entirely to her work, missing deadlines, losing assignments, and in one case, publishing an almost entirely fictitious exposé of the Marseille art world. (It speaks badly of that art world that even today it has yet to take notice.)

And yet despite all these mishaps, the journalism awards arrived. There was no stopping them. They came to J.T. the way flies come to honey, flus to Asia, and wealth to investment bankers. What did she think of these awards? She couldn't give a fuck, and in fact had said so a few times—in just those terms. The grand dame of New York journalism had a real mouth—one which was generally confined to three relatively receptive and forgiving venues: the editorial room, the street, and the reporter bars scattered across the world.

Success came easily to J.T. In part, it was because she was smart. Scary smart. But it was also, as she knew, because the game was rigged. Journalism felt like high school all over again, when she would just put her name on her assignments and receive her automatic "A's." She knew very well that all the teachers presumed her to be an A student and thus gave her an automatic "A." This was confirmed when, just to test the hypothesis, she scotched her homework assignment on Billy Budd and instead cribbed some lesbian erotica, turning it in to Ms. Devo in English class. "A" again. Clearly no one actually read her homework. (The thought that Ms. Devo might herself be a lesbian is not one that crossed J.T.'s mind at the time.)

After nearly two decades in journalism, the world, which had once seemed so enigmatic and exciting, had become familiar—predictable even. Which was shocking, given the cruelty she had witnessed on some of her assignments: Mogadishu, Chechnya, Darfur. J.T. was not indifferent or cold. It's just that having seen so much horror, perpetrated in the same way (over and over again), it had ceased to shock. A psychiatrist she met at a party once said that it was a form of PTSD. But she knew better: It was simply habituation, desensitization—or what the physiologists call adaptation. That and the fact that, as a journalist, she really couldn't do anything about it, except report. Reporting was not nothing, of course, but it fell short of the impassioned social engagement she had wished for as an undergrad at Yale. Plus, the job had its unseemly side: She constantly had to betray all these people just to get the story. She became their friend, sucked them dry for information, and then coldly shunted them aside for the sake of "the story." That's when she didn't betray them outright. To be a serious journalist required the development of a thick emotional exoskeleton. And she had one. So, PTSD? Not likely. More like advanced professionalism. Someday she would write about it all, but not before retirement was in sight—which, frankly, she doubted would ever happen.

J.T. thought of herself and all her assignments as simply going from one place to another. The problem, as she saw it, was that one place was always the same as the one before. She was supposed to get somewhere, and she never did. She never got there. She never left. It had become tiresome.

There was her love life, of course, which was varied and tumultuous—multicultural, multinational, and multigendered. Journalism, especially among foreign correspondents, had a way of curing monogamy and greatly expanding possibilities. But that sort of serial one-stop show was tiresome as well. She dreamed of a world-class romance, something torrid that would crack her soul and lay it bare, open, helpless—something on the order of Charles Zucker during those two years in Paris.

But Charles Zucker was a thing of the past. And now he had danced his last tango. Esophageal cancer, stage 3. Three months, maybe four at the outside.

She was feeling blue and jaded. Not the bluest she had ever felt, but certainly the most jaded. And so when the editorial office received this black hole of a tip, this nothing of a story, about people in L.A. just driving around for no reason, she told the editor, "What the hell. It's L.A. Of course they're driving around. Yeah, I'll do it."

The editor tried to dissuade her. "But there's nothing there!" he said. "There's nothing to be said about it."

"I know, I know. But that's the point. I need a challenge right now."

"Well, it's yours. Oh, and J.T.—I hate to ask you this right now—"

"What?"

"Can you do me a big favor and look up that young writer we just signed up, Michael Zelnack? The guy seemed so promising, and I haven't heard from him. See if he's got something for us. I'd like you to see him, just so he knows we treat him seriously here."

"What? We treat our young writers seriously now?"

"J.T.—knock it off."

"So anything I should know about Michael?" J.T. knew that her editor didn't do anything without an agenda.

"No. He's just not quite as productive as we thought he might be."

"Aaaaah."

■ ■ ■

And so, after lunch at Raison D'être with her literary agent, J.T. went in search of Michael Zelnack. When she called his cell, he didn't answer. Which for a writer was both strange and not: Writers are eager to get the news (answer the call!) and at the same time zealously protective of writing time (shut the damn thing off!).

J.T. got his voicemail. "Hi, Michael, this is J.T. The editor asked me to get in touch with you to see how things are going. You can reach me at this number. Not after midnight. Cheers."

It took a while, two weeks to be precise, but J.T. and Michael finally did meet one afternoon at Café Extra on the Upper East Side—one of those small neo-French bakeries with bleached wood floors and rustic farmhouse tables and benches.

J.T. favored double espressos. Michael went for a large 2 percent latte. J.T. had a croissant. Michael ordered a bagel. Small talk was had, but not for long.

"So, any stories you're working on that might interest us?"

"I have a couple of projects right now. Still finding my way."

"Subjects?"

"Professional culture."

"Specifically?"

"Interviews. Doctors, lawyers, bankers, consultants . . . everything."

"Storyline?"

"Delusion."

"About?"

"Self and others."

"Well, that just about covers it, doesn't it? So, you're not really into sharing, are you?"

"No, I like to keep the ideas fresh in my mind. I don't like feedback so much. It transforms my story. I'm very private that way."

■ ■ ■

Feedback from an old hand like J.T. probably would have transformed Michael's story. If he had one. Or if he was working on one. But he wasn't. Like half the New Yorkers he knew (mostly up and rising twenty-somethings), Michael was writing a book. He had been writing a book, the same book, for as long as he could remember. It was pretty much like the books being written by half of all the other people he knew were writing books. In truth, it was actually the same book.

In New York, there were only two kinds of books published at the time—a fiction book and a nonfiction book. The fiction book (which is not the one Michael was writing) involved family dysfunction—as recounted by a very omniscient narrator who nonetheless took the perspective of the various main characters to expose humorous, touching, and occasionally tragic thoughts and episodes that revealed deep (or talk-show worthy) truths about the human condition. The other book, the nonfiction book, was a memoir of how the author had encountered serious adversity leading to severe psychological distress but overcame it through meditation, world travel, religious revelation, romance, gratuitous sex, or something of the sort. (This is the one Michael was writing.)

Now, in truth, there were a handful of other publishers doing other kinds of books, but these were mostly small publishers who really didn't know what they were doing. The mainline publishing industry, from the heights of Farrar, Strauss & Giroux on down, focused on these two books—each of which came out every year, under different authorial names, in several versions, and all essentially the same.

Michael was an ambitious guy (like many of the other would-be writers), and he was determined to be (just as they were) The One to write The Book. Or more accurately, the one among the other several thousand who would also write The Book.

Like the other New York would-be writers, Michael also did "The Other Thing." The Other Thing was to take long walks around Manhattan thinking about what should go in The Book. This should not have taken so long given that everyone knew what should go in The Book. But it added to the aura of New York to have all these people walking around, talking to themselves in agitated states.

Tourists were not particularly good at picking out the would-be writers from the New York natives. But unquestionably, the would-be writers made New York more New York-like. And the natives could pick them out. That in turn made the natives feel more native-like. More like New York was staying New York and not being transformed into some generic version of itself. Unlike the west coast *parvenus*—with their slap-dash approach to questions of existential meaning—New Yorkers knew that identity was not something to be trifled with. They knew that in America, the tourist/native distinction went straight to the heart of the matter.

Michael's plan for The Book was not particularly extensive. He planned to start with adversity and overcome it. Elaborations would follow. Complexities would arise. One of the things that Michael had to decide upon (just like the other would-be writers) was how long it should take him to write The Book, how miserably poor he should be while writing it, and how much pain it should cause him.

Starting with the last first, the obvious question was how many girlfriends and friendships he should squander or otherwise betray during the writing period. Should his personal integrity itself be put at risk too, and if so, how badly should it be damaged? Finally, how much should he find himself psychically indebted to the bottle, to dope, or to some other addiction?

As to the question of how poor he should be, that was a tough one because he had actually come into a sizeable inheritance from his uncle Jonah, and he was not keen on wasting it. Faking poverty, meanwhile, was something he viewed as immoral, and he was not about to compromise that. So he struggled for a while with the poverty question.

As for how long it should take to write The Book, there were two schools of thought. There was the "boy genius theory," which held that The Book should be written as quickly as possible, thereby confirming the author's incomparable writing talents. In diametrical opposition was the "time is suffering theory," which held that writing The Book should take as long as possible, thereby evidencing the tremendous labor and personal sacrifice involved in bringing The Book into being. There wasn't much consensus among the New York would-be writers on which approach was preferable. There was, however, near-universal agreement that doing both at once or trying for the middle was extremely unwise.

Outsiders might have thought that there was no reason to consider any of these questions given that it was always the same book that would be published. But that just showed how little outsiders understood the New York publishing world. Indeed, the pain, poverty, and duration questions were, aside from the attire, accent, and affect of the author, among the most important things on which the writers established their brand identity.

Things had been going relatively well for Michael until the recession. At that point there was serious talk of moving away from the two-book model down to a one-book model. Ultimately, it didn't happen, but the recession did hit the publishing industry rather hard. A kind of neo-gothic gloom descended upon Manhattan. Publishing houses were "reorganized," editors were "reassigned," services "upgraded." Emails went unanswered, phone calls unreturned, lunch dates unfulfilled. Agents retooled. It was a bad time. The effects rippled down the various publishing hierarchies, from CEOs to vice presidents to editors to literary agents, to would-be writers, to the partners of the would-be writers, to their local grocers, to their car mechanics, and then back on up the hierarchies and on and on in the circular and endless way recessions always work. It was not pretty. Adversity and family dysfunction had never nestled so near to the heart of the publishing industry.

Michael, like the other New York would-be writers, responded in a positive way by resolving to do more walking around. Freed from actual writing, he felt liberated—not only in a literary but a personal sense as well. Michael's thinking ranged broadly along new pathways. He began to wonder, for instance, what the point of writing was if all the would-be writers were writing the same book. It was a puzzle. Most crudely put (and often this is exactly the way he put it): If everyone was writing the same book, why not have just one person write it? Why have thousands of would-be writers writing the same book?

There were obvious answers, of course. But none seemed wholly satisfying to Michael.

And then one day on 44th and 6th Avenue, as he was waiting for the light to change, he had an epiphany. He would write his own book.

His friends tried to talk him out of it. They got him drunk. They needled, cajoled, browbeat, and even tried to scare him. Susan, who was just a friend, even slept with him on the profoundly mistaken theory that it would make him more vulnerable and thus able to see reason in bed.

Everything was tried. Nothing worked.

Michael stood firm. He would write his own book.

Except that within a few weeks, Michael came to the realization that he was not ready to write his own book. He didn't know where to start, what to write, or how to do it. And so like many other New York would-be writers, who had also secretly tried (and failed) to write their own books, Michael dedicated himself to walking around New York full-time. He came to see it as his essential function and was actually quite pleased with himself. Indeed, he determined that walking around full-time made him an incomparably better writer—more lucid, more lyrical even, if he wasn't actually writing anything.

In this regard, Michael was, if not writer-zero, at least among the first to develop this new approach to writing in New York—namely, walking around full-time. It has to be said that, in this regard, the New Yorkers were somewhat behind their erstwhile L.A. counterparts. Indeed, while in L.A. the A-to-B thing was already in full swing, the New Yorkers were still wandering around. Much later, when historians and media critics would look back on this period, they would characterize walking around as a distinctly more primitive and anterior stage to going from A to B. But that is getting ahead of the story.

The Lawyers

After the incident on Santa Monica and Avenue of the Stars, John Morrison never saw David Madden again. There was no reason to. The offer of representation was silly, a momentary lapse. Besides, given that Morrison was himself now involved in the incident, he would be barred from representing David. Then too, John Morrison had never been to court. Plus he simply had too much work to do.

Or not.

It seemed to be both at once, depending upon the perspective.

On the one hand, John was assigned to an impressive number of deals. On top of the never-ending Aronson deal (the "undeal") he had been assigned to the Diamond deal, the Pascott deal, the Menshenk deal, the Freemont merger, and the Quanta acquisition. (There were more.) And on all these deals, he was routinely called upon by the partner in charge to write "contingency memos." Howard & Simpson prided itself on strategy and control. "We control the chaos, so you don't have to"—that was the epigram printed at the foot of their letterhead. The contingency memos were basically think and research pieces aimed at setting out beforehand how the firm would respond in the event of various contingencies—things that might happen in a deal such as the addition of a new firm, the disappearance of an old one, unexpected showings of interest by a government agency, financial status changes, and so on. The work was complex. But the structure was simple: If A then B, if X then Y, and so on. Since deals typically involved a great number of contingencies, and since Howard & Simpson believed in preparing "down to the third level," this truly was a great deal of work.

But in another sense, it was also truly not. It turned out, as John Morrison discovered after his first year with the firm, that no one actually read the contingency memos, that they never came into play. And so John Morrison had taken to simply recycling the old ones, changing names and figures if necessary and then, after a while, barely bothering to do that. It was a fairly mindless operation, and it was performed rather quickly.

This left him with a great deal of time for much of the day—time he spent listening to his music stream, doing crunches, or most often, staring blankly out the window at the traffic below. It had a tranquilizing effect, and John wondered whether, if he stared long enough, he could reach some kind of altered consciousness.

Having all this time meant that John's mind could go in all sorts of directions. Unfortunately for him, the most frequent destination was boredom.

Still, his approach had its rewards. His prodigious output did not go unnoticed. As John's billable hours peaked, the commendations from the partners kept coming: "awesome dedication," "unflappable professionalism," and "extraordinary contributions to the cause." The latter seemed a bit over the top to John, who had no idea just what "cause" it was he might be contributing to. These accolades culminated into John's early promotion to the coveted status of Tier 1 consultant.

John Morrison was asked stay on the Aronson deal, but to approach it from a Tier 1 perspective. In this new capacity, John's essential mission was to oversee, integrate, and facilitate communication among the various parties—the lawyers, the bankers, the accountants, the acquisition specialists, and so on. This oversight, integration, and facilitation is what Tier 1 consultants did *par excellence*—whether they were lawyers, bankers, accountants, acquisition specialists, or what have you.

As he examined the Aronson deal from a Tier 1 perspective, John figured out (and it did take him a while) why the deal hadn't moved forward in ten months of hard work. His conclusion was at once a surprise and yet incontrovertible: There were too many Tier 1 consultants on the deal. Somehow everyone—the lawyers, the accountants, the bankers, the acquisition specialists—had all staffed the deal with their own Tier 1 people.

The upshot was that everyone, or nearly everyone, was busy overseeing, integrating, and facilitating. This was part of the reason the documents kept going around in circles among the various professionals without anything moving forward. The lawyers said they wanted the accounting statements before they did anything. The accountants said they wanted the opinion letters from the lawyers before release of the statements. The bankers were unwilling to venture any estimates until they got the accountants' statements. And everyone was trying their damnedest to oversee, integrate, and facilitate.

This was bad enough. But then John traced out the full implications. And in one sudden, adrenalin-spiked moment, he realized that there really wasn't anything to oversee, integrate, and facilitate except everybody else's oversight, integration, and facilitation. There was, in short, nothing there.

He called his old corporations law professor at Harvard, who was completely unfazed. "Oh yeah, sure—ontological deficiency," he said. "No. That's just what we call it. We've known about it for years. So many deals fall through these days precisely for that reason. Everybody thinks there's a deal. Only there isn't because there are too many Tier 1 consultants. All you have is talk about a deal—and a lot of oversight, integration, and facilitation. But there's nothing there, so after a while, people get tired, pull out, and everybody thinks the deal fell through. The irony is that there was never any deal there to begin with. You would have thought business would be the last place for this to happen. Well, it's happening now."

"What do I do?"

"Nothing. There's nothing you can do. Inform the client."

John took the advice and called the Vice President in Charge of Deals at Aronson. "What do you mean, there's no deal?" John took the phone away from his ear. "You mean it's fallen through?"

"No, William. It's not that. It's just that—well there isn't any deal. There was never any deal. We're not really working on anything."

"Then what am I paying you for?"

"Well, we're working. It's just that what we're working on, uh, isn't anything."

The Vice President in Charge of Deals didn't respond. There was a long silence until John Morrison took up the slack. "William, I'm calling because I don't think you really want us to be involved in this."

"Wait. Back up for a second. We've been working on this deal for ten months now and you're telling me—have I got this right?—that there isn't anything there? Is that what you're telling me, John? Because I don't want to hear that, John."

"That's what I'm telling you."

"Well, that is totally unacceptable. What am I going to tell the CEO? The CFO? I am not hearing this. This is not happening."

Here it took some real courage on John's part. "But it is happening, William."

"Well, John, you're putting me in an awful bind here. How

can I possibly go back to my superiors and tell them that the deal we've been working on for ten months doesn't really exist? Just tell me, how do I do *that*, John?"

John pondered this and for the first time the full range of professional consequences lit up all at once on his mental screen—an evil constellation of catastrophes previously obscured but now shining very brightly, very large, and very close. The embarrassment alone (putting aside the subsequent litigation) would be devastating. Certainly Howard & Simpson would never be the same.

It stood to reason that everyone—the lawyers, the bankers, the accountants, the acquisition specialists—would, for the first time in ten months, have a clear and compelling common interest—namely, to preserve the illusion of the deal. They would all turn against him. They would flay him alive. Lawyer Carpaccio.

And so thinking all this, John decided that a touch of modulation, perhaps even a little walking back, might be advisable. Certainly, it was not good to have a deal fall through. It's not the sort of thing that one wanted to be associated with—fault or no fault. But it was so vastly preferable, so immensely more desirable, to have the deal fall through (which, of course, it would since it didn't exist) than to acknowledge that one had been working for ten months on a non-existent something. Philosophers made their careers on that sort of thing. Lawyers destroyed theirs.

"William, I may be being too hasty here. There's no deal right now, but that doesn't mean that we can't have one."

"That's my boy."

"So I'll just keep plugging away. Try to get us all on the same page. Now, I can't promise anything," he cautioned.

"Just give it your best shot, John. That's all I can ask." The Vice President in Charge of Deals signed off.

John leaned back in his chair and combed his hair. Having just averted a near disaster, he felt gratitude—boundless, undifferentiated, universal gratitude. He appreciated for the first time the extraordinary advantages of being a Tier 1 consultant. One was responsible only for overseeing, integrating, and facilitating. In the future, John would do nothing but Tier 1 work. In retrospect, it's fair to say that this was the precise moment when John Morrison realized he had truly arrived. No more of this A-to-B stuff. Henceforth, he would only go in circles.

Revenge Shopping

Eloise imagined great things for her revenge shopping. She planned. She considered. She strategized. Most people think that revenge shopping is relatively simple—a matter of buying whatever the offending spouse hates (hopefully something expensive) and bringing it home (hopefully in large quantities). But that's underwhelming. Lacking in force and gravitas—like putting on the Dixie Chicks when the occasion called for Mozart's Requiem.

Eloise understood these things implicitly. What Eloise planned to do was purchase items that David would have to accept as legitimate purchases (though he couldn't stand them) and feel bad about (whether or not they were returned). In addition, it would help tremendously if he understood that as much as he hated the items in question, she loved them. And it would be good too if the more she came to love the items, the more he would hate them. Eloise had an intuitive understanding of the dynamics of the feedback loop (though, of course, she would never have called it that). Finally, to drive him absolutely nuts, it would help if he understood implicitly, without her having to tell him (that was essential), that part of the reason she loved the items so much was precisely because he hated them so much.

This then was Eloise's plan of action. At the conceptual level, it was flawless. She had not done much revenge shopping in the past, and so she was proud of having produced such a stalwart action plan so quickly. The problem, however, and it surfaced almost immediately, was that while the concept was clear, it was also barren: Nothing came to mind. Somewhere between high concept and actual execution, the circuit had been blown. Visualization failed. Details remained elusive. Motivation started to falter.

The truth is she had come to accept The Affair. More importantly, she started to question her once-secure conviction that David was lying. Perhaps, contrary to what she had imagined earlier, it truly had been only once and long ago and almost an accident. (Well, not that.) And recently David seemed to be making a real effort to be present, attentive.

And then too she discovered still another one of those tiny dissident strains of thought from deep in the nether regions of her being. And it said, "This is wrong. This is not you." And though it was a tiny (tiny) strain, speaking softly (very softly) from a previously unidentified region, she could not put it aside entirely. Whatever the reason, her heart simply wasn't into revenge anymore.

This is not to say, however, that The Affair was entirely dead as a source of emotional sustenance. Eloise still had the bonding and the commiseration with her friends. Eloise had imagined that The Affair would give her new status in the group. It wasn't that she aspired to be the center of attention. She just wanted a bit more attention. Her share.

And she got it. From day one, the group was there for her—the five friends on the phone and then gradually the rest of the group. They listened to her complaints, empathized with her pain, and worried about her future. Twice they took her out to fancy restaurants where they all got lit, charged up outrageous expenses, laughed too loudly, returned dirty looks from the other guests, and generally had a grand time. (Trudy broke one of her high heels, and Rachel left her Visa behind—but these were acceptable losses.)

All in all, these evenings were greatly self-affirming even if on the morning after, the self in question wanted to slink off and drown its cluster headache in the bottom of a Bloody Mary and crawl back into bed or punish itself mercilessly on an elliptical trainer. One of the two. Possibly both.

If Eloise had majored in psychology in college (which she didn't), she would have learned that imbibing is basically the destruction of the bourgeois ego. This allows the id to party really hard all night long. In the morning, however, the self is left wholly unprotected from a superego keen to lead it in forced marches through swamps of guilt and shame (which, in all likelihood, that self richly deserves given the previous night's behavior).

Still, even considering this vexing zero-sum ratio, the fact remained that these raucous sisterly soirees provided Eloise real emotional sustenance. Succor was real and comfort lasting. Her friends were there for her. And that could not be taken away.

That is, not until her friend Maryann's baby was stillborn. At that point, the fountains of support, the outpourings of empathy which had all flowed freely towards Eloise were abruptly rerouted. Eloise too was expected to rechannel her attention towards Maryann.

It was an emotional pivot that caught Eloise off guard. It's not that Eloise was selfish or lacking in empathy. She could recognize Maryann's pain. It's just that Eloise was still suffering. She heard yet another small voice inside that kept saying, often at inopportune times, "Hey, what about me?" Eloise was ashamed of this voice. She knew in her better being, in her best self, that this little voice should be stamped out.

Still, whenever left untended, the *what-about-me?* voice bubbled up. And, of course, the main currents of pain, sadness, and anger had not entirely disappeared. In addition, there was the tiny dissident stream of relief and satisfaction that The Affair had finally happened. And muddying everything was Eloise's nascent suspicion that David might well have been telling the truth (or something close to it) in claiming that The Affair was long past. Altogether, Eloise was in a whirlpool of emotional turbulence. The only time she felt calm about the whole thing was after a few glasses of Chardonnay, and that obviously created epistemological problems of its own.

It was difficult for Eloise to sort all this out—to decide which currents to follow, which to dam up, and which to ignore altogether. She dearly wished she could talk to her personal therapist about all this. But that was not happening. In fact, it was repeatedly not happening: The therapist had canceled twice now. Once because of migraines. And once because she had an emergency request to pick up her nephew after school. Nephew? At school? Now, how likely was that?

The upshot is that Eloise, for the first time in a very long time, was going to have to sort out her emotional confusions all on her own. She could not talk to her friends. David was obviously out. And the therapist had gone AWOL. Eloise felt even more alone than on the day she discovered The Affair.

Not entirely alone, of course, because there was always the marriage counselor. But the problem with the marriage counselor was that she and Eloise no longer seemed to be on the same wavelength. Indeed, ever since the marriage counselor learned of The Affair, the marriage counselor had been downright chipper. She seemed genuinely happy to see David and Eloise at the sessions. When they arrived in the morning now, there were crullers and miniature croissants on the table next to the tea and coffee. The marriage counselor insisted, and David and Eloise agreed, that they increase their sessions to once a week on Thursday morning.

The term "process," which had been receding into the background, was now fully revivified and pressed into serious work-outs—as were David and Eloise, who received a one-page print-out describing "process exercises." Among the seven exercises on the list were a "fun list," an "intimacy exercise," an "advanced intimacy exercise," and a "what I like about you" minute. The instruction at the end enjoined the couple to do at least two exercises a day and to "*Have fun!*" Eloise winced inwardly as she imagined David's reaction.

First Session

"When did you first start having this sense that you don't have a real job?"

David pondered the question and couldn't recall exactly. "It came on gradually," he said. "At the beginning, I think I did go to the office. Certainly, that was true at my old job. But even with my new job, I think at one time, I did go. It's hard to remember. Anyway, even with the old job, I started going to the office less frequently. That's how it started."

"You consciously decided not to go to the office?'

"No. No. I'd go. I'd get dressed, get in my car, but I would never actually get there. In truth, I don't know where my office is located. And I'm not sure exactly what I do."

"But you get paid?"

This was a difficult question for David. As he thought about it, he became confused. "See, that's the thing. Recently, I've begun to think that maybe I don't really have a job. Like maybe I just made the whole thing up. You know, a defense mechanism, or whatever you call it these days."

The psychiatrist smiled. It was his first smile of the session. Like many male psychiatrists of a certain age, Dr. Ferrell cultivated an austere cerebral appearance. He had a graying beard with a severe cut—not unlike the well-known portraits of Sigmund Freud. Dr. Ferrell's cerebral aura was helped considerably by his high forehead, which he viewed (despite knowing better) as a sign of superior intelligence.

David was not answering the question. Dr. Ferrell considered pressing David. Dr. Ferrell wanted David to acknowledge that he had a real job (and got paid for it) or didn't have a real job (and if so, did not get paid). It was one or the other. To think otherwise would be absurd. But then Dr. Ferrell thought better of forcing the issue. After all, this was just David's first session, and given his obvious dissonance, better to feel things out gently.

"Defense mechanism—that's right, that's still what we call it," said Dr. Ferrell. "So, how does it make you feel when you think you have no real job?"

"Well, it ups the ante. It's pretty stressful for me to drive all day long—going from A to B. But if there's no job to boot, well, that's just additional stress."

"So you don't actually like all this driving around, as you call it? It's not rewarding for you?"

"Well, at first it was great. I enjoyed it a lot. But now, I find it stressful. The traffic and all. Plus it's become predictable too. I just go from A to B. It's like I'm always doing the same thing."

"Okay. Let me back up here. Let's deal with the job aspect first. So, every weekday, you get dressed and go off to work—is that right?"

"Yes."

"Yet you're not sure you have a real job?" Dr. Ferrell knew that this question might again plunge David into an uncomfortable dissonance, but Dr. Ferrell wanted to see how David would react.

Once again David became confused. His gaze started traveling. He looked away from Dr. Ferrell, towards the bookshelf, out the window, and finally up to the ceiling. He said, "I see what you mean. But that's why I'm here. I want to straighten things out."

"Let's try to get at it this way: When do you have these feelings that you don't have a real job, as you say?"

"When I'm bored. Mostly when I'm caught in a traffic jam. Sometimes before social occasions."

"Let's talk about the social occasions. What happens then?"

"I'm afraid people will ask me about work."

"And the other times when you're bored or caught in a traffic jam—what happens then?"

"Well, my mind drifts."

"So let me suggest a way of thinking about it: It seems fair to say that you associate not having a real job with some fairly negative experiences—is that right?"

"I guess."

"So, I'm going to ask you a difficult question—a hypothetical. If you did have a real job, how would you feel about it? Happy, unhappy, enthusiastic? What feelings come to mind?"

David didn't answer right away. Dr. Ferrell noticed David's eyes darting down and to the left. In his professional opinion, David looked stiff, uncomfortable. Dr. Ferrell determined that whatever David said next would, in all likelihood, be untrue.

"I think I would feel relieved," David said.

"Okay. Very good. Our time is up anyway. The good news is I think I can help you."

"But I have another problem."

"Well, perhaps we can discuss that next time."

"I'm famous, you see and—"

"Well, congratulations."

"No, no. I'm famous in a bad way. I'm the guy who—"

"Well, I *am* sorry, but I have a patient waiting."

Dr. Ferrell rose from his chair and instinctively David did the same. They shook hands, and David trudged out.

After David left, Dr. Ferrell's assistant walked in—Tella, a young woman with a streak of magenta in her hair and a tiny green dragon tattoo on her left shoulder. Tella suffered from borderline personality disorder and Dr. Ferrell, who charged a small fortune for sessions, had accepted her part-time receptionist services in exchange for therapy and a very small salary. Over the years (two now) they had become good, strictly platonic friends. At times, there had been a tinge of father/daughter ideation, but otherwise it has been an extremely healthy relationship.

"So whadaya think?" she asked.

"Garden variety depressive. Detectable paranoid ideation, mild social anxiety, and a block of unknown etiology. Can't really tell yet. I'll have to keep a watch. He's afraid he doesn't have a real job—even though every morning he heads off to work. Says he's famous."

"So what are you gonna do for him?"

"Help him adjust. What else can I do? Tella, these professionals—these lawyers, bankers, accountants, doctors—most of them can't stand their jobs. Can you imagine coming in every day to do a job you loathe? Wouldn't you try to do all you can to avoid it—psychically, at least? This guy's just like the rest except that he's basically into a much more severe form of avoidance behavior."

"So what exactly do you do in this case?"

"I'm going to help him accept the life of quiet desperation he has chosen for himself. That plus 20 milligrams of Prozac twice a day. That's what I do, Tella—help ease our patients into accepting circumstances that are ultimately intolerable." Dr. Ferrell's voice dropped as he looked out the window and sighed.

"You do know who he is—don't you?"

"Should I?"

So Tella showed him a copy of *The National Gazette*. There on the cover of the tell-all weekly newsprint magazine was the photograph of a man apparently relieving himself on the edge of a sidewalk in some urban setting. It was David. His offending anatomy had been photoshopped out of visual existence.

Dr. Ferrell stroked his chin—smoothing out his imaginary beard. "Uhm," he said, thoughtfully. "I see. I see."

Media Coverage

How David Madden made the cover of *The National Gazette* was something of a fluke. It was not KZLA 9News that did it. To be sure, the news team did show on that day. But once they arrived, there wasn't much to report. There were two well-dressed men sitting on the sidewalk in handcuffs. The TV crew took a video, and it did air on the five o'clock news, but it was not much of a story.

So David's misadventure would have been entirely forgotten but for the intervention of a freelance photographer. The latter had been awaiting the arrival of Noelle Giscard, bad girl extraordinaire, at her lawyer's office in Century City when David's misadventures occurred. The freelance photographer witnessed the whole thing—from the moment David relieved himself by the curb all the way to his arrest and the bizarre accident with the little red sports car. The photographer took roughly forty to fifty frames, one of which was used as the cover of that week's edition of *The National Gazette* along with the headline: "Man Causes Epic Traffic Jam."

David was famous.

Mariana could not have hoped for more. Her little accident with David's car was going to pay off. She had planned it all along, of course. She had wanted to make contact, to insinuate herself into his life—and what more direct and reliable way than crashing into his car? They would need to talk about insurance estimates, arrange a fair price. They would haggle. He would protest. She would give in. Her charm would win him over. And if not that, then her business acumen. She would become his publicist. And this had cost what—twelve hundred dollars to Trish's red Miata and a couple of thousand to David's car? Peanuts. Meanwhile she had a new client. And already he was famous.

Mariana's first impression of David was generally positive: A reasonably well-to-do middle-aged man. Tall with a blunt and honest face. She thought she detected a little Scottish or Irish blood. He seemed genial enough given the circumstances—the accident and all. Most important, he was, in her professional opinion, malleable.

Mariana still had no clear idea what she could do with David, but that was exactly the point: She wanted a challenge. Various possibilities crossed the mental screen: A trial, a protest. *Think big,* she told herself. It had not gelled yet.

Mariana took a sip of her second two-percent, extra-hot morning Americano and wondered about the lawyer yesterday.

Rakish—a bit young. Could she use him? Would he be part of the story? She didn't know yet.

Reader Response

When "L.A. Unsustainable" came out, J.T. didn't pay much attention. She was working on another article and had moved on. But she did pay attention to her response comments because some of them were a bit shocking:

> *"Total academic B.S. The New Amsterdam now relies on dissertations!!!!???? You don't name a single driver in your article. How does this get past the editors?"*
>
> *"That was a complete snow job. I know Tony White. I went to school with Tony White. He was totally nuts then, totally nuts now. Can't believe you write this crap."*
>
> *"So people are just driving around. They're going from A to B. BFD! Who cares? It's L.A. What else do you expect? The Chamber of Commerce guy was dead on."*

Some of it, of course, was the usual flattery:

> *"Wonderful flow. Lyrical even. And how interesting. Who would have thought?"*

And some of it was tangential:

> *"Only in L.A."*

And, of course, a lot of it was clinical:

> *"The government is funding lots of similar projects. There's a reason we haven't heard about this before. I am Jesus."*

Overall, the most shocking thing of all for J.T. was just how few response comments she received. She had thought that (as usual) she would hit a nerve. At the very least strike within the periphery. No go. The readership apparently took a pass. There was no press follow-up. The blogs (putting aside the usual conspiracy sites) showed no real interest. At best, the article was an also-ran.

Maybe they were right. Maybe this wasn't a big deal. Maybe she wouldn't get the Charles Zucker Award after all.

Her editor tried to console her but didn't do a very good job. He said the article was too abstract—too much about ideas, not enough about facts.

She had tried to explain it to him. "It's not about *facts*. That's the problem with these people—they're abstract. They just go from A to B. They're leading lives of . . . of dissipating abstraction!"

"J.T., we're in the magazine business. You know that. I know that. Ideas don't sell."

"But it's not about ideas! It's about form—abstraction."

"Well, we don't do abstraction! And we certainly do not do *dissipating abstraction*. What the hell is that?" The editor didn't get it, and J.T. reproached herself for getting defensive. At her age, with her accomplishments! Inappropriate—really. Still, for one split second, J.T. thought about quitting and retiring to the summer home in Dubrovnik that she had yet to purchase for herself.

■ ■ ■

Among those within the L.A. therapy community, some clients took a strong interest in J.T.'s piece. But it's safe to say that the overwhelming majority did not. Among those therapy clients who had actually read the piece, many just didn't care. Some had real jobs (and were quite sure of it). Others had much bigger emotional problems to address (and priorities to meet). Still others had pleasantly adjusted to their driving habits (and dismissed Tony White out of hand as yet another left-wing academic snob).

As for the therapists themselves, they too had different reactions. David Madden's psychiatrist did subscribe to *The New Amsterdam* and did read the piece. It provoked some new thoughts. Dr. Ferrell considered that he might have been wrong about David. Perhaps David was in fact one of those drivers described in the article who just went from A to B. And perhaps David was right in thinking he didn't have a real job.

These considerations prompted Dr. Ferrell to revise his overall view of David Madden's case. If David didn't actually have a real job, then his case became far more pedestrian—so pedestrian, in fact, that Dr. Ferrell (whose expertise was in great demand) might not be needed at all in such a routine case. Considering all this, David's therapist began to wonder whether terminating therapy might not be appropriate.

Which is precisely what he suggested at the next session. "I think we need to consider terminating therapy," he said bluntly.

"But this is only my second appointment!" David exclaimed.

"Well, yes, but after reflecting on your situation, it seems to me," said Dr. Ferrell, "quite conceivable that you don't have a real job."

"But that's horrible! I need therapy."

"No, on the contrary. If in fact you don't have a real job, then it seems to me that you are well on your way to adjusting to that reality. I don't think that there's anything for me to address here—no underlying pathology, no obvious dysfunction."

"But what about my driving around?"

"Well, yes, currently you are. But you're probably still at an early stage in the acceptance process. Frankly, I don't expect it to last. So, I think you should feel pretty good about everything. Extinction will soon set in."

"What do you mean, extinction?"

"Oh, that just means you'll very likely stop driving around. Think of it as a scab on an injury. Sooner or later, it falls off."

"Then what?"

"Well, then you'll be unemployed."

"But that's terrible."

When David left Dr. Ferrell's office, he felt like he'd just been fired. Maybe twice even. First the therapist suggested he might not have a real job. That was bad enough. But then the therapist unilaterally terminated David's therapy. This did not seem to David like standard operating procedure—particularly not for a person who had obvious insecurities about whether he had a job or not.

Still, this was David's first real encounter with therapy (putting aside the marriage counseling, which he didn't consider therapy at all) and so he wasn't sure. Intuitively, however, he felt that it was very likely the patient's prerogative to decide when to terminate therapy. Probably Eloise would know.

■ ■ ■

Eloise's therapist—the one Eloise never saw—probably would not have liked J.T.'s article. If she had read it. Which she didn't, because that sort of thing was no longer part of her universe. Eloise's therapist saw herself as a dedicated professional which, to her, had come to mean that she drove the sort of car that a well-to-do Brentwood therapist might drive. In her case, this meant a lustrous, deep racing green Acura TL with a moonroof and a cream leather interior. It was an impressive car with only 7,238 miles on it. The sort of car that a well-to-do therapist would drive.

She fondly recalled buying the car. In a matter of weeks, she had become an expert on the various specifications, colors, interiors, engine types, models, accessories, and features of various high-end cars. Of course, she knew nothing about the mechanics. Nor did she appreciate the significance of the various metrics on which she had become an expert. (But she did know that, as a general rule, bigger, higher, and more is better than smaller, lower, and less.) And in the end, she decided this meant Acura.

She went from A to B in style. This was her essential function. It's what therapists of true stature did. And she liked it. Cruising down San Vicente to the beach. Turning right at 7th Street through the curves down to U.S. 1. Going all the way up to Malibu and then back down to Sunset past Palisades, past Brentwood, through all those banked curves to arrive at UCLA. Then down to Beverly Hills. Then Century City. Back up Benedict Canyon. This was the life. This was L.A.

■ ■ ■

Eloise did read J.T.'s article while waiting at the dentist's office (cavities in 18 and 19). Eloise thought the article was really weird. She quickly became convinced it was one of these New York-L.A. one-upsmanship things. Among the reasons Eloise could think this was that she had never been to New York. (Additionally, she also hadn't seen much of L.A. besides the West Side.)

Eloise would have liked to talk about the article with her therapist because, among other things, Eloise had begun to wonder whether David might be anything like the drivers in the article. It's not that she knew for sure. But David occasionally did mention his various driving excursions—to downtown, to Hollywood, to Santa Monica. Driving here and then there. And if one added them all up, one couldn't help but think that the man did a lot of driving. How could he find any time to work?

■ ■ ■

Michael Zelnack, like most New York would-be writers, read *The New Amsterdam*. Since he didn't get it online (there was always that damned delay), he simply lifted it from the kiosks. It had to be done. For a New York would-be writer not to read *The Amsterdam* was like walking naked in the streets. It's not that *The Amsterdam* was any good—New York would-be writers never acknowledged that anything was any good (that would be professional suicide). Rather one needed to read it because . . . well, if one didn't, it was kind of hard to put it down. New York was not like the Midwest, and writing was not football. You couldn't just step into a bar in the East Village and say, "Well, how about that last issue of *The Amsterdam*?" You needed something a bit more cerebral—something with attitude, edge, focus.

The trouble was that Michael actually liked J.T.'s article. Worse even: It had actually occurred to Michael Zelnack that the L.A. drivers' experience could, given sufficient metaphorical license, be likened to the behavior of the New York would-be writers like himself. The idea was definitely a stretch and surely unacceptable to Michael's cohort. Still, the thought wasn't entirely bereft: The L.A. drivers drove compulsively from A to B while the New York would-be writers walked compulsively to nowhere in particular.

True—it wasn't exactly the same thing. But viewed from a strictly philosophical angle, there was a certain existential affinity among the two—namely, a certain dearth of meaning to the two activities.

Even as he repeated it to himself, Michael knew his analogy to be heretical. Sufficiently so that he did not tell anyone—save Susan, who was sleeping with him regularly now (reason apparently having dropped out of the picture entirely).

None of this precluded Michael from expressing certain caustic views on the work of J.T. who, in addition to being the personification of the New York publishing hierarchy, seemed to think, much to Michael's irritation, that she was his immediate (real life) supervisor. At the Bloody Angst Bar & Grill on the Lower East Side, Michael held forth in a subtly contrarian way to a coterie of fellow writers—a gay couple from Delaware, a threesome from Dublin, and, of course, Susan. "Nothing is easier than to ridicule L.A." pronounced Michael over a pint of extra special bitter. "Why even bother? The place satirizes itself. Poof."

"But I thought you liked the article," said Susan.

"Well, the writing—"

"No. You said you really liked it, Michael."

Michael looked at Susan and realized she didn't understand the situation and would not let up.

"Okay. So I liked the article," he said sheepishly, expecting all manner of verbal abuse, professional assault, literary epithets, and, if the three Irish literary henchmen across the table consumed enough whiskey, possibly some sonnets of unimaginable cruelty.

All at his expense. It was going to be the pits.

"I said I liked it, but not in the usual ways."

"You liked it in unusual ways then—hey mate?" asked one of the men across the table, a wicked smile on his face.

Yes, it was going to be the pits.

The Action

David, though he had no idea at the time, would soon be thrust to the forefront of what the press grossly mislabeled as "The Action." The first public manifestation of The Action was heard on KFOB, "All weather, all traffic, all the time." Apparently, over the past month there had been a net 400-plus percent increase in the number of traffic jams due to stalled cars. The overwhelming majority of these cars had inexplicably run out of gas. The drivers did not seem to have any explanations. It did not seem intentional. They generally seemed to be confused about where they were going. Or why.

Particularly worrisome was that some of these cars managed to stall in the middle of the freeways. The 405, the 10, the 45, the 56, the 210, 310, and 382 were all home to some spectacular accidents. No deaths, but several serious injuries. And, of course, epic traffic jams.

Eagle News Network was the first to detect a pattern. Tom

Bates, host of "American Patriot," devoted an entire show the day after the KFOB report. Bates framed the issues at the outset: "Ladies and gentlemen, we have, at this time, no direct information that The Action was carried out by terrorists. At the same time, it would be irresponsible to rule it out." And then Tom Bates directed a question to his first guest: "Let me ask you this: What explanations do we have for The Action? What reason is there for all these cars to stall at once?" This was followed by a second question: "Are these drivers related in any way? Do we have any word from Homeland Security on that?" And then a third: "Now assuming, and I'm not saying this is true, but assuming The Action is part of a terrorist attack, what can we expect to happen next? And what can we do to guard ourselves against it?"

After "American Patriot," all the networks started referring to the stalled cars as "The Action." The brooding omnipresence of terrorism was never far off-screen. The aura of threat was kicked up a few notches when the president visited L.A. on the occasion of the men's World Cup Soccer finals at the Rose Bowl: His limo was immobilized for four-and-a-half hours. The incident was covered by cable news. All three networks showed live clips of the stranded presidential limousine. Experts and pundits were assembled in real time to discuss whether this could be the initial step in a terrorist plot.

The Republican House Whip came out blaring: "The idea that the leader of the free world can be immobilized, frozen in place like this, is unacceptable. The president should never have let this happen." Deborah Milstein, a professor of Middle Eastern Studies at Georgetown University and perhaps the most balanced of the experts, opined that it would be extremely unusual of Al Qaeda or any affiliated groups to use traffic jams to isolate a target. "Too unreliable. And it's not one of their SOPs," she said. The white-haired anchor then said, "But you can't rule it out, can you, Professor?" One of the pundits noted that it was premature to rule out Al Qaeda. Perhaps the most bizarre statement was made by a caller into "Super American Patriot" (also Eagle News Network), who suggested that the 25th Amendment (the provision pertaining to presidential incapacitation) should have been invoked.

The number of stalled cars multiplied. The LAPD reported that the vast majority of these cars were all inexplicably out of gas. The local networks and the *L.A. Times* ran editorials requesting the city council and the mayor to initiate investigations. The drivers were interrogated by the police, but nothing came of it. The Los Angeles Chief of Police held a press conference: "We do not, at this time, have any basis to hold these drivers. Nearly all of them expressed regret for the inconvenience. And when interrogated, nearly all said they could not understand why this happened. In these circumstances, we cannot do anything. We have no evidence whatsoever of any concerted action or conspiracy."

The KZLA reporter was particularly aggressive. "But they shut down the city twelve times in the past month! Fifty to one hundred stalled cars on the freeways and the city comes to a grinding halt! What do you plan to do about this?"

"We're doing all we can. We are trying to get to the bottom of this."

"Is this some kind of protest? What do they want?"

"Again, I repeat, we have no evidence at this time of any concerted action or conspiracy. We're looking at this as hard as we can."

"There have been reports of public urination. Can you comment?"

"That was just one isolated case—the *National Gazette* case."

"Are there any planned prosecutions?"

"You'll have to ask the district attorney on that. Okay. One last question."

"Is there any truth to the rumors that the FBI or Homeland Security will relieve you of jurisdiction at this point?"

The chief leaned back and sighed. He looked to his press secretary, all the way to the right of the room, and smiled. "We have received no information to that effect."

■ ■ ■

Mariana turned off the TiVo as the Chief of Police walked away from the lectern. "You see, David," she said, turning to him on the sofa, "this has people really concerned, really upset. We need to get out in front of this thing."

"What thing? It's just a bunch of people who ran out of gas. Just like me. That's what the Chief said."

"David, that's not the way things work in media. Stuff happens. Weird stuff. Normal stuff. Any kind of stuff. And we turn it into a story—no matter what it is. Think about it: What do you see on the news every night? I'll tell you: Accidents, murders, natural catastrophes, adultery, war, famine, and terrorism. Is any of this news? Of course not. It's stuff that happens all the time. Somewhere a government is being toppled. Somewhere else there's a bomb blast, a sex scandal, a killer storm. Is any of it really news? Of course not. There is nothing new about it. It is *always* like this all the time."

David listened attentively. Mariana was emphatic, her gestures large and sweeping, her voice loud and excited for such a small woman.

"So why then do we watch the news?" she asked. "Why do we care?" She paused for a few seconds. "It's the story, David. The story—that's what matters. And the question is: what story do we want to put on all of this—the driving, the A to B, the stalled cars? What do we want to do with it? That's the question."

"You mean we decide?"

"Only if we're good and fast enough."

"But I don't have a story."

"That's where I come in. Tell me about the A-to-B stuff. I want to hear about that. Is that like the *New Amsterdam* article I gave you?"

"Who is J.T.?" David asked.

"Just a reporter."

"She writes well. And she has the A-to-B thing down pat. But she doesn't get the frustration. For her, it's just fun. That's what it used to be like for me. But that was long ago. Now, it's kind of stressful."

"So how does all this stress make you feel, David?"

The question reminded David of his marriage counselor.

"It makes me upset," he said.

"That's good, David. Very good. Now, what about it all makes you feel mad?"

The "feel" word triggered more thoughts about the marriage counselor.

"I get tired of talking about how I feel. It never goes anywhere."

"Well, yes. But I was talking about the A-to-B stuff—that doesn't go anywhere either, does it? Doesn't that make you mad?"

"Well, a bit, I suppose."

In the lengthy give and take between Mariana and David, they came to a meeting of the minds—mostly Mariana's mind, actually. As Mariana saw it, David was mad about this A-to-B stuff never getting anywhere. And as Mariana suggested to David, it wasn't just him who was mad, but lots of people. "We're all mad," she said.

She really had to tug at David, however. The anger modality did not run deep in his emotional repertoire. She persisted. She prompted, teased, cajoled, and provoked him until he could do an almost convincing imitation of that great indigenous American figure—the unreconstructed angry white man. Mariana had studied the style at Stanford—the Klan, the know-nothings, the Birchers, the moral majority, the Christian fundamentalists, the

Tea Partiers. Slightly different orientations, same underlying social pathology: A stream of inchoate anger stretching back to the antebellum period and extending into the future as far as the eye could see. It was deeply engrained in the national psyche—the sort of thing a publicist could really count on.

David, meanwhile, wondered why Mariana was trying to get him all upset about the A and B stuff. Certainly, it wasn't pleasant, but he didn't want to make a federal case out of it.

She did, however. Mariana wanted to go national—capitalize on the lead of the *National Gazette*.

"We'll get you on the talk shows yet," she said, as she punched his shoulder affectionately. "For now, we'll start with local news."

■ ■ ■

KZLA 9News, generally at the forefront of local politics coverage and human interest stories, gathered several of the stalled drivers for a group interview. The anchor, Bill Desmond, asked, "Is this a protest? What do you all want?" They said they didn't want anything. They were sorry and just wanted to get on with their lives.

"But you stalled your cars on the freeways. You produced massive gridlock. You literally shut down large portions of Los Angeles not just one day, but by my count, on fifteen separate occasions! The governor was considering bringing out the National Guard."

"Well, we're sorry about that. We just forgot to fill our tanks."

"And you expect the American people to believe that?"

The drivers looked around at each other and nodded.

"Yes. We do."

Then one of the drivers, Mr. David Madden, raised his hand and said, "We're really kind of stressed about all this. It makes us feel . . . We don't think it's right that, uh . . ."

"You don't think what's right?"

"Being stressed," he said.

The anchor's eyes lit up. A live one. Finally! A story! Something!

"So you're stressed—angry. I think what our viewers want to know is: What are you angry about?"

"We're always just going from one place to another. From A to B. It's all predictable." David looked around for support.

"Yeah, we're predictable," said another driver. "We *are* predictable," echoed another one.

David continued, "We don't want to be predictable. There's got to be something more. We think there is."

Bill Desmond felt the first few drops of sweat seeping down his shirt collar. He was in one of the few professions on earth (politics and floor-trading being the other two) where you actually had to spray anti-perspirant directly on the neck. Obviously, he'd forgotten. Getting these drivers to say something (anything) was like sucking sap from tree bark. One more question.

"Nearly all of you ran out of gas during the day. Where were you going? You, sir, over here."

"I was going from A to B."

Bill Desmond began to think this was going nowhere. Had he been an intellectual, he might have been amused that the storyline of his drivers (not going anywhere) was being inscribed in his own storyline (also not going anywhere.) But Bill Desmond was not an intellectual. He was a news commentator. And so he was not amused in the least. "And that's a wrap. Mark—back to you," he said to the anchor.

■ ■ ■

"How'd I do?" David asked Mariana, hopefully.

"It was a disaster, David. A total freaking fuck-monster of a disaster. I'm not sure I can help you. At all."

"What'd I do wrong?"

"You're not angry enough, David."

"But I'm not trying to be."

"And that right there would be our problem."

Mariana became contemplative, thoughtful. She'd have to come up with a different hook. The angry white man thing? Totally fucking not happening.

The Conference

The Thomas Hadley Memorial Hall of U.C. Berkeley was nearly two-thirds full. This meant an audience of roughly 120 to 150 people. It also meant, by academic standards, that the conference was a rousing success. The assembled academics—lit crits, sociologists, law professors, a few philosophers, some grad students—were talking feverishly in groups of two or three. It was the beginning of the conference, and these people were not called the vanguard of the chattering classes for nothing.

In a paper delivered in this very hall some twenty years ago, one of Marshall McLuhan's students had once argued that most conversations in Western culture fell within five fundamental forms: intellectual exploration, wit, gossip, intimacy, and information exchange. He added that of the five, academics were exceedingly active with regard to the first three, generally awkward as regards the fourth, and almost congenitally incapable of staying on topic with regard to the fifth. All in all, the upshot was that they talked a lot. A whole lot.

At five past nine, Max Stein, the Charles M. Fairmont Professor of Cognitive and Rhetorical Studies at U. C. Berkeley, rose from his seat and walked to the podium. He cut an elegant figure, with a thinning shock of white hair and a piercingly intelligent smile. The audience became quiet. Max Stein was holding a sheaf of yellow lined note papers. He stood behind the podium grasping both sides as if he owned it.

He looked out at the audience, scratched his neck, looked out at the audience again, smiled broadly, and then, with an air of genuine bemusement, said, "It seems, uh . . . I have had to revise my views." The audience broke out into raucous laughter.

"Somewhat," he added, smiling.

"All the way, Max!" someone yelled from the back.

More laughter.

"Alright. I'm referring, of course, to the Tony White thesis. It is my honor and privilege as one of Tony White's many unrestrained fans, and his former thesis adviser, to welcome you all to our conference, 'Meaning (and Not).' I think it's safe to say, we all arrive here on the brink of two searingly critical questions. First, do we suffer from a great surfeit of cultural narratives or not nearly enough? Second, is anyone listening?"

Dirk Thompson, a newly appointed assistant professor in rhetoric at Princeton, was definitely not. He was far too busy scouting the audience from his vantage in the second row. He was looking for a date for this evening.

Max Stein straightened out his sheaf of papers on the podium, looked to the ceiling as if there were something really interesting happening up there, appeared to get lost in the detailed patterns of the fiberboard, the asbestos, or whatever it was, and then recovered. He said, "Let me start with the second question. The answer is clear: No one is listening. Rather than argue that point, I will use my time to explain why no one is listening—mindful, of course, of the fact that we, on the left, have always been too good at explaining the failure of our own theories. As for the first question—too much narrative or too little?—well, in the end, it amounts to the same thing, doesn't it? The real question is, what should we do about it?"

Dirk Thompson, who caught the last bit, groaned quietly to himself. Metaphorically raising his hands in biblical anguish to the sky (or the fiberboard), he asked himself, *Must we hear this overcooked deconstructive nonsense yet one more time? Please, dear God. And must we hear that ridiculous political question on top of it: what should we do about it? Well, it's obvious what we should do, isn't it?—launch the revolution from the interstices of the conference proceeding papers! Resist at the margins of the university press book! Let a thousand endnotes bloom! Aaaaargh!* Dirk Thompson was convinced that this older generation would never go away. It would publish its transgressive artifacts well into its collective Alzheimers. It would write provocations and manifestos from its sickbeds. It would issue interventions from its retirement homes. It would be heard from in hell. Along with The Airplane, The Dead, The Stones, The Whatevers, which would all be playing simultaneously nonstop all the time. As far as Dirk Thompson was concerned, the world has never seen such a generation as this, and it was to be fervently hoped that none such would ever be seen again. Whenever he was agitated (and this was such a time), Dirk's upper lip would quiver, and his pleasantly plump cheeks would glow with a suggestion of blush. To say the man looked cherubic would be a stretch, but not by much.

In any event, Dirk Thompson had no patience for this sort of academic blather. Actually, when it came down to it, there were only three things that really interested him, albeit intensely so. The first was his cultural studies project, which was called, somewhat enigmatically, "Toothpaste." The second was frequenting world-class restaurants such as Chez Jacqueline (where, thanks to reservations made almost three months ago, he would dine tonight with some as-yet-to-be-specified someone). And the third was the hopefully endless line of women (colleagues, students, and others) he intended to bed in the indefinite future. (Generally one at a time, though he had previously enjoyed and remained open to other arrangements.)

"One of the questions that I think we will need to address, even if not answer, at this conference," Max Stein said, "is whether the A-to-B structure is problematic because it never stops—the so-called 'compulsion thesis'—or whether it is problematic because it never leads anywhere—the so-called the 'nihilism thesis.' The question is important because it influences what, if anything, we can do about it. In other words, do we want to get beyond A to B? Or do we simply want to make sure A to B gets us somewhere?"

"I want to mention that Tony White is here and . . . " The room exploded into applause. "I also want to say I have prevailed on him to serve as conference *rapporteur* at the end." More applause. "I also would like to make a pitch for one panel discussion in particular. It will be an 'author responds to critics' format. Except that it will be actor responds to critics. We have with us Mr. David Madden." Again the room erupted with applause.

"Thank you."

■ ■ ■

On the king-size hotel bed on the fourth floor of the Fairview Hotel overlooking the bay, a woman was spread out in well-earned abandon. Max Stein stroked her thigh lightly with the back of his hand. *She's still quite beautiful,* he thought. Striking, composed—more confident now than at twenty-five when every boy in school wanted her. And back then they were together. So why didn't they stay together? And why was such an important choice left up to a bunch of self-involved twenty-somethings with a criminally short horizon span like them? He would really like to know, but instead he asked, "How did you get onto the Tony White thing?"

"Well," she said slowly, turning over on her stomach. "I was already doing the story on the L.A. drivers. That actually came into the office. It was an honest-to-goodness assignment. But the Tony White thing I heard about later. By accident. It was a dinner party on the East Side—literati, intellectuals, post-docs, editors, canapés, caviar, blah, blah, blah. I was flirting with a boy from Columbia who was trying desperately to impress me with his ideas. I still don't know whether he was trying to get an internship or take me to bed. It's hard, you know, when you're famous."

"I know," he said.

"Anyway, most of his ideas, I later discovered, came from Tony White. I downloaded the thesis, skimmed it, and decided to give Tony a call. This was way before The Action or any of that stuff."

"Why did you take the assignment in the first place?"

"Literary challenge, Max. Literary challenge."

"I don't get it."

"And you, of all people! I wanted a challenge. Reportorial, literary—whatever you want to call it. Could I actually write a piece that had as its subject and its overarching narrative this ridiculously abstract formula: getting from A to B? Apparently, the answer was yes, I could. Looking back, I had no idea what I was getting into. Still, absurdity is a great premise. All the normal rules are on holiday. As for me, as usual, the devil was in the details."

"I don't believe you. You're too much the journalist. I think the devil was in the extrapolations—the panoply of ideas surrounding this metaphor—from A to B."

"Max, you're so the academic. So silly. A to B is nothing. Or maybe it's everything."

"Increasingly so, I'm afraid."

"You plan to say that this afternoon?"

"I plan to say as little as possible. I'm exhausted. Plus, conveniently, I'm no longer on your panel. I'm on with David Madden."

"Exhausted—intellectually?" And then a stray thought: "Physically?" she asked with alarm.

"Both. Add emotionally too. You have no idea how much I dread these conferences. How much I long for one of these bright young things from Harvard or Yale or Stanford to say something—anything! Anything at all. Anything that doesn't sound like somebody's homework assignment. I swear, if I have to read another one of these cultural studies pieces, I'm going to write on the performative significance of flossing in the liminal spaces of the 1890's Appalachian imaginary. I really will. How did we manage to recruit so many intellectual dust bunnies? How did we make them?"

"Are you ready to go yet?"

"You're venal."

"I try."

"No, you're a natural." Max reached for the water glass on his bedside table. "So: was I ever the one?"

"I don't think I ever met a one for me. You were close. But once I turned seventeen, I thought there would never be just one. You?"

"You could have been the one. No. I'm lying. You would have been. I was a fool," he said.

"You're not listening. You actually spared yourself a lot of pain, Max. Besides, we were all fools."

"Maybe so. You know, I've been thinking about death lately."

"And?"

"Well, I'm annoyed. One of my friends—I don't think you ever knew Charlie. Anyway, he was killed two months ago. He was sixty-one. It was, as they say, a freak accident—sailing on Lake Washington in Seattle. But the man had a great life. Sixty-one. And I was thinking, so he missed out on another fifteen or twenty years. I mean, it's sad for family and friends. But it is going to end for all of us, right? It's not like you can beat this thing. So he misses out on those extra years. So what? If you think about it, he's also going to miss out on thousands of years after that. Hell, he's already missed a lot. The Battle of Hastings. The Peace of Westphalia."

"I can't believe the distance you take."

"No, no, this is totally grounded. I'm not being cold. I loved the guy. I'm just trying to look death straight in the face. I mean, I think the hardest thing about death from one's own point of view is not death, but the things that go with it. Like watching a loved one. Or dying too young. Or seeing it coming. That's all horrible. But philosophically? The thing that's hard is not death. It's the idea you only go around once. And so at some point, you look around and you say, this is my life. This is what it's been. This is my partner. These are my kids, and this is my work. This is what I've done. This is it. I was around, and this is what I've been."

"Regrets?"

"You. But otherwise, no, not really. I've said what I wanted to say. Done what I wanted. All in all, I'm pretty happy with it. It would be nice, I suppose, if I'd been born ten years earlier—then I wouldn't have to watch the moronic self-immolation of this country. But even then, you know, taking the long view, it doesn't really matter."

Max put his arms behind his head and yawned.

"People think we progress," he went on. "The ratchet theory of history. That's silly. People are always going to fuck up. And they're always going to do some incredibly heroic things too. Basically, it's like one endless baseball game: Some beautiful innings. Some really lousy ones. But in the main, it's mostly incredibly long periods in between where nothing's happening and people are just sitting around waiting. It's not like there's an end to the story. There's not even a single timeline."

"You're becoming quite the stoic."

"Yes, but with a sense of humor."

"Actually, I think I have it all wrong. Just never mind," he said, reaching for a glass of water.

"Hey, I could use that," J.T. said. "Which reminds me: I'm doing a follow-up on 'L.A. Unsustainable.'" It's almost all done. I've just got to integrate the conference. Can I have an interview with the great Max Stein?"

"J.T., you don't need an interview. You know what I think before I do."

"So I can write up anything? I can have you say anything I need for the piece?"

"Yep. Anything you want. Just be nice. Mind you, I'm not ready to retire just yet."

■ ■ ■

"I want to welcome you to this panel," said Max Stein. "I will serve as moderator. As I said yesterday, this will be an actor-meets-critics session. I need to apprise Mr. Madden that 'critics' in our context means 'literary critics' and that it's extremely unlikely anyone will actually criticize his performance." Scattered laughter, a few giggles—it wasn't all that funny, but it was meant to put David at ease. And more importantly: to signal to everyone else that David was off limits.

"So our first panelist . . ." Max Stein issued the usual vastly over-inflated introduction. The first panelist, a somewhat disheveled young man with a healthy post-adolescent beard, took the podium.

"Public urination," he said, "occurs for sundry reasons, across cultures, and in different contexts. Its meaning is plural, dispersed, and coded. For too long we have tried to impose a singular meaning to what can only be taken as a polymorphous act."

He went on with great exuberance, stroking his beard. He didn't have that particular academic gesture down yet; too deliberate, insufficiently pensive. His delivery, however, was pitch perfect.

"What we need to remember here," he concluded, "is that

public urination is first and foremost a performance."

The Judith Butler fans in the audience applauded.

Dirk Thompson took out his cell phone.

The second speaker was a small round woman with a cowlick and oversized earrings. She flipped her hair back brusquely and started speaking in a tough, gravelly brogue. "Okay people, we need to get our act together. This was no ordinary public urination. This was a wake-up call. It was motivated, directed, and fraught with significance. Mr. Madden, here is the proverbial canary in a coal mine. What better . . . and here I ask you for a moment's reflection . . . what more fitting primordial protest can nature offer against the artifice of culture than the eruption of this raw, unmediated biological need?" She pounded the podium. "We need to see Mr. Madden's act as the rebellion of a subjugated nature against an alien and oppressive cultural domination."

The Judith Butler fans booed.

Dirk Thompson winced inwardly. *What do you mean, we need to see?* You *need to see.* I *don't need to see anything.*

Next up was an apologist, obviously a token presence included for balance. Apologists in the academy are known for being blunt and to the point. This one—a bullish man with a crewcut—was true to form. "I wish to take exception to the two prior speakers. We all know from the great Scottish philosopher David Hume that were it not for causation—A causes B—life would just be one damned thing after another. Viewed from this perspective, the fact that Mr. Madden, like countless citizens in this great country, can *actually* make A yield B is something to be cherished, not condemned. As for Mr. Madden's act, L.A. Municipal Code 41.47.2 says all that needs to be said on the subject."

Up until that last line, the apologist would have been doing not great, but okay. He would have received polite even if perfunctory applause. As it was, the last line did him in, bringing boos from the audience. Which, of course, is what the apologist both expected and intended—a fact fully confirmed by his smile and the waving of his notes as he squeezed by the panelists to go sit down.

When it came time for David to respond, the room became eerily quiet. The aura of a monastery.

"I'm very flattered to be here," he said. "I do want to say that for me, and I've been told by Max Stein that I should speak frankly, I just . . . well, I was in a situation where I really felt forced. There was really no choice, no option."

The two Marxists in the audience started clapping, but as they had discovered a certain incompatibility at lunch (one was a Trotskyite, the other a former member of the RCP), each immediately ceased clapping when he noticed the other doing so.

David continued, "It's true that I am not happy with this A-to-B thing never getting anywhere." During the conference that phrase had become a kind of mantra: this-A-to-B-thing-never-getting-anywhere. At one point, some of the speakers started referring to it by its acronym, TATBTNGA (pronounced "Tab-Naga").

"But I don't think my act had all that much to do with this-A-to-B-thing-never-getting-anywhere. It was just one of those things. I thought about it on the Southwest flight on the way up here: It's important to keep the two things separate. Anyway, I hope this helps you. I want to tell you that this is the first time I've been to an academic conference. I think you guys have great jobs, even if I don't understand much of what you're saying."

The Judith Butler fans wanted to boo, but knew better.

"Wait, wait, wait," said Max Stein, rising to his obligations as moderator. "We have time for some questions from the audience. Yes, the gentleman in the back there."

"I guess what I'd like to know is whether you've resumed your activities—you know, driving from A to B? Are you back to that? Are you satisfied?"

David blinked. "I would say, definitely, that it's not the same as before. I haven't run out of gas, if that's what you mean. But sometimes, I'm unable to follow through—to actually get to where I'm going. There are times when I find myself driving, and I've forgotten where I am supposed to be going."

"What happens then?"

"Usually, I try to retrace my steps. I go back to where I've been. But lately, that's sometimes a problem too. I get confused."

Max Stein cut in again. "You, sir, in the red shirt in the middle there."

"Is there a medical angle to all this?"

Groans, smirks, and sighs. Max Stein cut in again: "With all due respect, we had an entire panel on that yesterday. Okay. One more question."

"May I?" said the panelist from U.C. Irvine, raising his hand to interrupt. "I want to comment on Mr. Madden's last statement—his inability not only to get to where he's going but also to get back to where he was. You see, this thing, it builds on itself. First, Mr. Madden just drives around from A to B, figuratively speaking. Next he's not able to drive around because he gets confused. And now he can't even retrace his steps. What we're seeing here is a gradual but degenerative breakdown of essential functions. This is only the tip of the iceberg."

The panelist from U.C. Irvine rather obviously wanted to go on, but Max Stein deftly cut him off. "Okay, and on that note, I think this is a good place to end. Please join me in thanking our panelists. Oh, and tonight's reception starts at seven o'clock—after our guest speaker and *rapporteur*, Tony White, gives his summation. Thank you."

■ ■ ■

Later that afternoon, when Tony White took the stage, he received a standing ovation. There were even a few whistles. The man was a rock star.

One man wearing a red T-shirt and a much abused straw hat started chanting, "Tab Naga, Tab Naga, Tab Naga."

"Thank you," Tony said. "Thank you. I am honored to be here and to serve as your conference *rapporteur*. That is an impossible task: I cannot possibly sum up this conference. But I can highlight some of the main themes, which is what I intend to do. I'm mindful that the title of this conference is 'Meaning (and Not),' but I have decided here to focus on our discussions of the Madden Act.

"I've listened attentively and with great interest to all your interventions. The interpretations of the Madden Act, as we have begun to call it here, have been diverse and thought-provoking. Some of you have suggested that Mr. Madden was protesting a world of out of balance—a world single-mindedly and neurotically committed to going from A to B. Others have suggested that the root problem lies in the ubiquity of our own addictive inclinations—an inability to do anything other than go from A to B. The Heideggerians among you suggest that this is yet another an instance of the forgetting of being. Still others have argued that we have produced an essentially febrile population—one unable to resist the pull of even the dumbest patterned behavior. Some of you in the post-colonial tradition have suggested that Mr. Madden's act is a testimony to the decadence of the West—its inability to express nuance, subtlety, and difference. Still others have argued in the psychoanalytic vein that we have destroyed the ego. According to this line of thought, our only choices, figuratively speaking, are reduced to an inhuman superego symbolized in Mr. Madden's case by the dark towers of Century City or to an unrestrained id signified by his public urination."

Tony looked up from his scratchings on the yellow-lined paper. His dark, deeply recessed eyes swept left and right.

"Here, then, is my view of the matter. You don't get it."

The room fell silent. The shock and consternation were palpable.

"No," he said. "You don't get it. When I wrote my dissertation, I was trying to get people to see. To really see what was happening. With all due respect, it seems to me that what you've been doing here is what Mr. Madden is concerned about. It's just more of the same. You're just going from one place to another, from A to B, while ending up in the same place. The important thing is to be able to see. But none of your theories can help you see. You all end up wherever you start. Everything you encounter—including public urination, apparently—confirms to you what you started out with. You try to get from A to B. But your B is no different from your A. Only you don't see it. You think you're going somewhere. The thing is, you're not. All you're doing is internalizing other people's A-to-B, never-getting-anywhere-thing into your own A-to-B, never-getting-anywhere-thing. It's like one Russian doll inside another. Only you don't realize it."

And so it was. Two days of intense debate, confrontation, discussion, hallway talk—and it came to this! In any other conference, outrage would have been vocal, intense, and instantaneous. Figurative murder would have been a likely reaction. But this was Tony White. *The* Tony White.

Challenges, rebuttals, or calls for explanation being out of the question, the collective mood settled on despair. The conferees shuffled out—withdrawn, defeated, bovine. They were silent. The men brushed off their coats. The women nervously adjusted their skirts. They left, hands in pockets and arms crossing chests.

They said goodbye. "Tab Naga, dude."

They would all make their way back to their respective institutions—back east, down the coast, or back to the Midwest. They were deflated—not so much confused as uncomprehending. Their hero had rejected them. They all shed their sophisticated academic armature—their poststructuralism, their psychoanalysis, their post-colonial theory—and reverted back to a crude and long discredited humanism: Why had he done this? For what reason?

No one got the chance to find out. Tony was last seen in the company of a young woman, headed out the door.

■ ■ ■

Dirk Thompson's date had not shown yet, but this did not stop him from ordering. He selected a modest Entre-Deux-Mers to go with the fennel-laced oysters on the half shell. The wine was arrestingly sharp. The oysters, flown in from Amsterdam, slipped sumptuously down his throat, thus ending their long transatlantic journey from the North Sea.

His date still had not shown, and Dirk Thompson was now suffering from the mild pangs of an incipient annoyance. He ordered a glass of Puligny Montrachet 1998 to tide him over and perused the menu. The choices were as enticing as they were daunting.

Ten minutes later, his date was still not there. His annoyance prompted him to think again of the conference, which had the predictable effect of further fueling his irritation.

He ordered another glass of the Montrachet. He took small, delicate sips and listened to the carillon of the diners' silverware clinking on their plates. The choreography of the silverware along with the hushed contemplation of interiority (primarily oral) betokened the aura of a religious ceremony. As he sipped his wine, Dirk Thompson noticed yet another of Jacqueline's specials being served at the adjoining table—petit medaillons of tortured lamb with *sauce madeire*.

Since he had the time, Dirk Thompson decided to order another drink—this time a Bela Frappe made with Czech Absinthe. That turned out to be a mistake. The Bela Frappe was too sweet. The bartender had exceeded his sugar mandate.

Dirk Thompson called the waiter and politely requested that the glass be taken away and another Bela Frappe brought forward—this time with less sugar.

"*Mais bien sur*, monsieur. Right away."

But "right away" was not right away, as it turned out. Dirk snapped his fingers at the waiter—a gesture that prompted a number of the patrons to turn around.

"Where is my drink?"

"I am sorry, monsieur. Right away."

Dirk Thompson reached for the menu again but accidentally hit his water glass. As he reached for it to avert spillage, he miscalculated and sent it shattering onto the floor. Dirk Thompson could feel the uncomfortable heat of embarrassment flushing his face. Why on earth did these waiters insist on placing glasses so close to the plates?

The waiter hurried over, saying "It is nothing, monsieur."

"What do you mean, it's nothing? I've been waiting here for my drink, and it's still not here."

"*Tout suite,* monsieur."

No, this was too much. Limits had been breached. Boundaries broken. Chez Jacqueline charged amazing prices, and for that, amazing service was required in return. And that was clearly not happening. At least not to Dirk Thompson's liking. He normally would have considered his options here and chosen a deliberate course of action. But by this point, the three glasses of wine plus the Bela Frappe had taken charge. An unpredictable combination on the best of days, the concoction did little to contribute to Dirk's emotional equilibrium. On the contrary, it magnified a number of Dirk Thompson's frustrations. First the conference itself. A complete bust, that was. Then the late date. Chez Jacqueline not good enough, maybe? Really? And then on top of all that, the insolence of this incompetent waiter—an insolence that, when viewed through the clarifying prism of the wine and the absinthe, was really more in the way of an insult. An outrageous insult actually, if one wanted to take it that way (which Dirk did). And thus it was that pride was awakened and suitably supportive emotions mobilized.

If Dirk had thought about it (and he really was well beyond

that at this point), he would have recognized that alcohol and pride are symbiotic—each serving as a multiplier for the imperatives and demands of the other. As the limit is reached, the multiplier effect approaches the exponential—and that is precisely where it was when Dirk, in a fit of rage, slammed his fist on the table, sending the other glass of water flying and shouting, "This is an outrage!"

At that point, he was politely asked to leave—which he did, stopping by the bar to insult the bartender and to throw bills on the counter in payment for what he had already consumed.

His date never showed. Indeed, she never had any intention of showing. Dirk Thompson had a rep. Everyone knew.

■ ■ ■

The following morning Dirk Thompson took a long, hot shower. He shaved and slapped his cheeks. He looked in the mirror and was faced with the dull and vicious look of a person in the visceral clutches of an epic hangover. Which is precisely the way he felt—the headache, the rumbling stomach, the discombobulated intestines, the torpor of the musculature, the creaking of the joints. All bodily functions were reporting depletion and injury—all simultaneously demanding protein assistance, oxygen baths, vitamin saturation—lord god, something, please!

Dirk Thompson made a point of dressing in his best clothes—a white shirt, slacks, and linen sports jacket. He believed that this sartorial effort—particularly the fresh white shirt—had a way of countering the effects of the hangover, or at least shortening its life span. It was a bizarre belief, and it had no physiological basis. But he stuck by it, and it seemed to work as well as anything else.

Fully dressed and once again a force to be reckoned with, he returned to the bathroom to brush his teeth. As he squeezed out the green-streaked translucent toothpaste—an Italian import—he was reminded of his current work in progress—"Toothpaste."

He had, in the classic cultural studies genre, explored toothpaste from all sorts of angles—genealogy (the first dental cleansers were made with crushed bone, eggshells, and oyster shells); history (a British subject by the name of Peabody was the first to introduce soap to make dentifrice in 1824); aesthetics (color, taste, aroma, texture); semiotics (squeezing vs. rolling); the *de rigueur* sex chapter (the fetishism of toothpaste and the pleasures of orality); and three or four others.

The work was almost finished. He had a contract with a prestigious east coast university press. The book had been incredibly easy to write, formulaic even: Pick some radically underinvestigated cultural artifact (i.e., toothpaste) and then, chapter by chapter, submit it to an excruciatingly intense examination from every disciplinary approach conceivably applicable. It virtually wrote itself.

And now he needed something new. It occurred to him that this Tony White guy—the artichoke commune guy—might well be worth a little attention. Maybe it would be interesting to live in a commune for a while. At the very least, he would be able to luxuriate in the splendor of the Bay area instead of wasting away in suburban New Jersey.

From

The New Amsterdam Magazine
Dep't. of Cultural Affairs

The Academic Beat
By J.T.
January 30

Few people attend academic conferences. Among the least likely is Mr. David Madden, the man responsible for what has come to be known as the "Madden Act." At a recent conference at U.C. Berkeley, however, not only was Mr. Madden in attendance, he was the prime topic of discussion.

The conference, titled "Meaning (and Not)," brought academics and experts from all corners of the university to consider the state of meaning in contemporary America. Foremost on everyone's mind at the conference was the recent recognition that various generally accepted activities—going to work, writing novels—might not be as meaningful as previously thought.

As widely reported in the popular press, Mr. Madden has been at the forefront of this new learning—not only because of the notoriety of the Madden Act, but perhaps more fundamentally because he was one of the first to suffer from what is now generally called "the breakdowns"—the literal or figurative incapacity to perform simple tasks such as driving from A to B. Mr. Madden was among the first of the hundreds of L.A. drivers who inexplicably ran out of gas in the past several months.

I had a chance to speak with him the day following the conference.

"You've now become a public figure, Mr. Madden.

What do you make of all this?"

"Well, I was very flattered to be part of the conference. But, you know, I think these university professors were a bit too focused on the Madden Act. That was just something that happened. If it hadn't been for the location and the *National Gazette* photograph, it wouldn't have been such a big deal."

"Perhaps we can put the Madden Act aside and focus simply on the breakdowns. What is your understanding of the breakdowns?"

"I don't know. It's mysterious to me. There's a lot of commentary going on. A lot of TV coverage. It's really unsettling. We just don't know anymore. Everyone has been trying to get from A to B, but what we're discovering now is that they're not really getting anywhere. Every B becomes just another A—so what's the point? It's like me. I was driving from Venice to Downtown, and then Downtown to Los Feliz, and Los Feliz to the Wilshire District. But why? Why this incessant need to drive from A to B? That's the question."

"You feel like you weren't going anywhere?"

"That's right. I'd go from A to B and then B would turn out to be just another A. So why do this?"

I pointed out that Scott Daubert, a representative of the L.A. Chapter of the Chamber of Commerce, supported this activity.

"Well yeah, sure. But he doesn't have to do all the driving, does he?"

I asked Mr. David Madden whether he felt up to being a spokesperson for his generation.

"Various people have tried to push me in that direction. It's not something I'm comfortable with."

At the conference I had once again a chance to speak one-on-one (see "L.A. Unsustainable," *The New*

Amsterdam, Oct. 21) with Dr. Max Stein, who opened as keynote speaker. Dr. Stein, who is the Charles M. Fairmont Professor in Cognitive and Rhetorical Studies at U. C. Berkeley, is nothing if not emphatic.

"What we're seeing here, all across the country, is a breakdown in the fundamental cultural logic. It started in L.A. There were all these drivers going from A to B for no obvious reason. And then we started getting breakdowns. Obvious breakdowns like running out of gas. Mr. Madden was among the first, but hardly the only one to experience this.

"Then we discovered that it's not just driving. The driving breakdowns are mostly an L.A. thing. But we have breakdowns in shopping, work, education. Even here at the university."

Dr. Stein, who is often demonstrative, became visibly excited.

"And we're finding that the breakdowns aren't just limited to the A-to-B thing. The people who are going around in circles are starting to have breakdowns as well. It started with the Tier 1 consultants—you know, the consultants who consult on other consultants.

"And then, we're also finding that the people who go from A to A are having trouble. I understand that your industry, New York publishing, is a prime example. We're finding that increasingly writers have stopped writing. Instead, they just walk around trying to look like writers. And now, we find some who can't even do that anymore."

"What were the most promising explanations at your conference, 'Meaning (and Not)'?"

"Frankly, we have no shortage of explanations," Dr. Stein replied. "The psychologists say there is kind of blockage—performance aversion. The conservatives talk about a loss of values. The liberals talk about a rigged game and unequal outcomes. But all these people are simply doing their own shticks. They're basically processing the breakdowns through their own narratives. They're still doing A to B, or A to A, or going around in circles. On a fundamental level, they don't get it."

"Where is the younger generation on all this?"

Stein frowned. "I'm not sure. The thirty-somethings are nowhere to be seen on all this. I'm in my sixties, so I find it kind of sad. These thirty-somethings—they're basically very nice people. But they seem to approach life like a soccer game: 'What position do you want me to play?' Or like homework: 'What ideas do you want me to have?' It's a lost generation. It's our fault: We trained them. We did this to them."

Tony White, who originally detected the breakdowns in a dissertation, was also at the conference. In fact, it's fair to say that up until the penultimate moment, he was a rock star. I caught up with him at a café on Shattuck in Berkeley and asked him about his impressions.

"Well, to be perfectly frank, I found the whole thing really disappointing," he said. "As I explained in my wrap-up, they just don't get it. I think the person who came closest was the man from U.C. Irvine who said that this is the just the tip of the iceberg—the guy who said we're all meta-faking it."

"Meta-faking? I didn't hear him say that."

"I'm pretty sure he did. Maybe he said it on another panel. In any event, the point is: We're faking the faking. We're even faking that. That's meta-faking to the second power."

"Well, what do you think he meant by 'faking it'?"

"I can't speak for him. It's unfortunate he went over time and that Max Stein cut him off. But my guess is this: We've got lots of people industries—advertising, law, academia, medicine, real estate. These are all people-intensive. And what's happened is that somehow the culture has learned, on all sorts of levels, that it is easier to deliver an image of the goods than to supply the goods themselves. So everybody fakes it. They fake being a lawyer, a professor, a physician. Which at first is okay because the fakery is just as good as the thing itself. At first."

Tony raised his index finger in warning.

"But now, it's gone metastatic. And you get people who fake faking it and people who fake faking faking it. And then pretty soon you have nothing. Just people driving around—like Mr. Madden."

"But isn't that what Mr. Madden complained about?"

"Exactly. That's how the breakdowns start. They realize they're going from A to B. And then they ask the 'Why?' question. Or they start wondering what's so great about B. Or they start wondering why B always seems to turn into A again. And then, like Mr. Madden, they wonder where it's all going. And then one day, they can't do it anymore. Hence the breakdowns. They get confused. They're unable to carry on. They literally and figuratively run out of gas." Tony reclined in his seat, obviously pleased with his analysis.

"So you don't think the man from U.C. Irvine was faking it? " I asked.

Tony laughed. "That's very good. You're starting to get it."

"So there's more?"

"Sure. Lots."

"Such as?"

"The writers in New York. They used to write the same book. Or the same two books, right? And then many of them started simply walking around New

York. Soon they were doing it full-time. Many of them think that's what it is to be a writer these days—you just kind of walk around, talk to yourself under your breath, and try to look like a writer. Except the thing is, it's not working anymore. These people are having breakdowns too. It's really interesting because these are hard-core New Yorkers. They know their city. And yet lately, they go on their walks and then become so disoriented they can't even move. Breakdowns. Don't get me wrong: They know where they are—Grand Central, West Village, uptown, whatever. But they can't make the connections. They can't move because they don't know where anything is relative to anything else. Show them a map of Manhattan and they'll say 'yes, yes, yes.' Take it away, and they're lost again."

"We didn't hear anything about this at the conference, did we?"

"No, but as I tried to say at the end, the academics have their own problems."

"You've seen academic breakdowns?"

"Not personally, but it's happening. And not just academia. It's happening all over: Phoenix, Chicago, Boston, New Orleans—I monitor all this. There are some news stories. Not many, of course."

For the first time, in speaking with Tony, I was truly surprised. I had not seen anything yet in the national news outlets. All the stories of breakdowns were confined to L.A. (and the resulting traffic jams). Nothing else had surfaced. When I checked, however, a pronounced pattern of isolated postings on the net and local news stories confirmed Tony White's account. Breakdowns were happening across the nation, albeit not always in the same numbers.

I asked Tony whether there was a pattern to the breakdowns.

"Oh sure," he said. "In every case I've come

across, the breakdown is specific to the essential function being carried out. Hence, with the L.A. drivers, they run out of gas. With the New York walkers, they become disoriented. In Phoenix, at the strip malls, people are literally incapable of parking their cars. I have to say, if the same kind of thing weren't happening anywhere else, it would simply be unbelievable. I mean, how hard can it be to park a car? But can you imagine? In Phoenix—if you can't park a car, what can you do?"

"International?"

"I would watch England, frankly."

"Why England?"

"A predisposition, don't you think? I mean as countries go. They have a head start."

"Let's move on to Max Stein. I understand you have reconciled?"

"Yeah, we've talked. He apologized to me, and we're on the same page now. Same chapter at least. I think that apart from Mr. Madden, he probably comes closest to seeing what's happening. But you've really got to see. And I don't think they were doing that at the conference. You notice the entire conference dropped Max Stein's original question—do we have a surfeit of narrative or not nearly enough? Nobody touched that. Nobody."

"Why not?"

Tony chuckled. "It's because the answer is obvious: Of course we have too much narrative. Way too much. We're awash in narratives—the pundits, the politicians, the talking heads, the lawyers, the therapists, the talk-show hosts, the academics, the experts. They are the unacknowledged poets of our time. All our institutions, all our professions, are producing narratives like crazy. It's just that none of the narratives are any good."

"Why not?"

"Well, once you strip away all the detail, the jargon, the idioms, they're kind of all the same, aren't they? And pretty thin too."

I left Tony White at the café. For days afterwards, I searched for a way to summarize the conference. But with each new effort, I came to wonder whether, like the academics, I too wasn't doing my own A-to-B shtick. Is that what we are all doing?

The Philosopher

The day after the conference, Max Stein took off—up the coast on US 1 towards Mendocino and points beyond. As he drove into the Russian River valley, he thought of visiting Tony at the commune but passed on the idea. Max had to work. To get some thoughts down. Which lately had become difficult. It wasn't really a case of writer's block. Of this Max was certain. He knew writer's block. And writer's block knew him. Indeed, they were on intimate terms.

And why shouldn't they be? After all, they were both Max: Max 1 and Max 2. There was Max 1 to whom ideas came easily enough, and there was Max 2 to whom no ideas came at all (save occasionally the idea that no idea was good enough).

Though Max dreaded writer's block, he also thought there was a certain honor in it. As Max saw it, the onset of writer's block was a confirmation of his seriousness, his intellectual prowess, his commitment. Indeed, as he had declaimed at more than one Berkeley dinner party, "How could any academic worth his or her salt not experience writer's block?"

So this was not writer's block, though it belonged to the same general constellation. The truth is that for a year and a half now, the only time Max could write anything worth a damn was when he was roaming the West (preferably the great empty spaces of Wyoming or Utah). He would wander from town to town, coffee house to coffee house, dirt road to dirt road.

The "Nomadic Syndrome," he called it. And at this very moment, he was well within its force field—heading out on the open highway where imagination ran free and thoughts arrived. The important thing was to get them all down before they vanished or the inexorable gravitational pull of his work at Berkeley drew him back to the Bay Area.

Max was working on his opus—*Meaning (and Not)*, to be published by a British university press. The project was going okay—at least when Max was cruising the rutted dirt roads of the West. Just north of Salmon Creek Beach, the first thought came to him. He stopped at the next picnic area and powered up the laptop. He typed:

A Preliminary Inventory (A to B):

A to B—(progression)
A to A (stasis)
A to B which becomes an A for another B, etc. (serial repetition— neurosis)
A to B followed by B to A (circularity)

A never get to B (futility)
A to nowhere (nihilism)
Why B? (skepticism)
What B? (radical skepticism)
B to A (contrarianism)
A/B (gnosticism)
ABABABAB (schizophrenia)

As Max looked at the screen, he couldn't help but think it was all a tad too schematic, a bit too abstract. But that was the point, wasn't it? Everyone was leading these abstract and schematic lives caught up in the forms . . . that were themselves meaningless . . . but which everyone endowed with meaning . . . just as Max was doing right now as he mapped the permutations.

Max's laptop drifted off into sleep mode. Max himself was drifting off into sleep mode. He yawned. He needed an espresso.

Focus! he told himself. Now why go from A to B? Once again the screen lit up.

Because B is better than A (progress)
Because we're fated (destiny)
Because we're hardwired (human nature)
Because we so choose (existentialism)
Because that's what our people do (sociology)
Because we have false consciousness (Marxism)
Because no one has yet thought of anything else

Oh, what's the use? he wondered. The preternatural ease with which these patterns came to him was immensely disheartening. The permutations were so obvious. More distressing though, and Max could see this coming, was that the number of permutations was not endless. It was, once one got down to it, a rather small number. And all of human existence was contained within this limited set—flitting from one thing to another. And that just looked like more A to B. It was these stark realizations that kept Max from ever finishing the list.

And so it was this time as well as Max turned away from the screen to watch the great Pacific waves come in, one after another, each of them repeating the same pattern, the same curl (over and over again). Each wave reaching up gradually towards the heavens only to come crashing down in an explosion of white froth, then diffusing itself into nothingness—so that eventually each molecule of water would be severed from all its companions until once again, it would make common cause, reach for the heavens, and . . .

Oh what's the use! Max felt the sickly onset of dejection. And then in a flash, he realized that he was working on something that (if one could put Nietzsche aside) had yet to be conceived—had yet to be thought! Max was mapping the structures, the very forms, of the meaningless. This realization came to him with the full force of an epiphany—the kind of ecstatic transport that Max lived for.

Who else had mapped the forms of the meaningless? Nobody—that's who!

Of course, ecstatic transport does not last forever. And so it was this time as Max realized that it was the structure of *the meaningless* he was mapping. "Do you get that?" he rebuked himself. (This was no doubt Max 2 needling Max 1.) "Do you? Huh?

You—yes you—are dedicating your life to the philosophy of the meaningless. Do you think you could find maybe something more meaningless than that?" (Truth be known: Max 2 had an unpleasant propensity for sarcasm.)

But even Max 2 was not entirely irrational. Even Max 2 had his thoughtful moments: "You know it's one thing to say that shopping or professional sports or something in particular is meaningless. But if everything is really and truly meaningless, then what is there to be said about it—philosophically speaking?" (Max 2 clearly had a point here.) "Wouldn't finding meaning in the meaningless be paradoxical? In fact, self-refuting? And if one were to write an authentic philosophy of the meaningless, wouldn't fidelity require that one approach meaninglessness on its own terms, in its own idiom—which is to say meaninglessly?" (Max 2, like Max 1, was an adept dialectician.)

It was these kinds of thoughts—these incredibly abstract, arcane, schematic and paradoxical thoughts—that kept Max roaming the great empty spaces of the West. For one thing, roaming the West helped him make headway (mini-epiphanies in Landers, Wyoming; Escalante, Utah; and Burns, Oregon). For another, the great emptiness of the western desert filled Max's soul. Or so he believed.

But none of this was any good. Max thought he would like a juicy hamburger. With fries. And a pint of IPA.

The Upgrade

When David and Eloise arrived for their Thursday counseling session, the crullers and the miniature croissants had been replaced by lox, bagels, and cream cheese. The accoutrements included lemon, shallots, and capers. David had an uncomfortable feeling about this.

He was not keen on continuing the marriage counseling and had told Eloise exactly that earlier that morning.

"Hon, I just don't think we need it anymore."

"Well, I think it's hard to know, don't you, hon?"

David wanted to say that he did know. That in fact he was quite sure it was not necessary. But he also knew that this was not the way to approach the thing. Eloise would get back up. And then it would take another two or three months before he could broach the subject again.

"I think we could take a little break and see how it goes," he suggested.

"The counselor says continuity is everything."

David took a chance: "Aren't you a bit tired of processing everything? I mean, we could spend the time doing something else."

"Like what?"

"Like, I think we should fool around more often."

"Why don't we explore the idea with her?"

"No! I do not want to talk with her about that."

"I meant the processing."

That's where they had left it this morning at breakfast. Now here they were in the marriage counselor's office with the lox, bagels, and cream cheese.

David actually liked lox, but he was not fond of the marriage counselor's office. The drapes were excessively frilly. And the cream upholstery on the sofa had those little pleated skirts that flared at the bottom. It was not unattractive, but it seemed to David more appropriate for a tea salon than a marriage counselor's office. Then too, the room seemed to ooze dowdiness—as did the marriage counselor herself, who was always wearing cream yellow or beige-colored suits. Plus, she put on too much foundation and carried too much jewelry. The whole affect of the place was less marriage counseling than it was menopausal coffee klatch. Since David did not think of his wife as menopausal (or even near-menopausal) the affect, on the whole, was kind of a downer.

David also had a sense that this feminine interior decorating was not entirely fair to him or his gender. It was not neutral, and David felt that, where marriage counseling was concerned, the thing ought to be dealt with on neutral ground. He imagined more angular furniture, some metallic file cabinets, and hardwood chairs. He realized that this was not entirely neutral either. But then again, the marriage counselor being a woman—she really had to offer something in the way of a counter-balance. At any rate, as soon as David stepped into the marriage counselor's office every Thursday morning, he invariably felt outnumbered.

The bagel, lox, and cream cheese (despite its plausible appeal to the male of the species) did nothing to assuage his doubts about the whole enterprise. David, who always felt on guard at these Thursday meetings, immediately assumed that the bagel, lox, and cream cheese presaged some more substantial change.

And indeed it did.

"I have something really exciting to discuss with the two of you."

"Really," Eloise said, sitting up.

"Yes. I don't know where to start, so I'm just going to plunge right in. I've decided to upgrade my practice from marriage counseling to life consultant."

"Oh," said Eloise.

"As far as we're concerned, I will continue to advise on the marriage, but in a more holistic way."

"Holistic?" said David.

"Well, yes. We'll still be focused on you two as well as the marriage, but we'll do it from a much broader perspective. The idea will be to integrate everything—you, David, and the marriage—

into a rewarding experience for everyone."

The idea of integrating everything (her, David, and the marriage) was modestly appealing to Eloise. What was pleasing about the new approach is that finally they were going to move from "processing" to what seemed like a more promising activity—namely, "integrating." Processing, after all, was something that could go on forever. Integrating, by contrast, had a very different feel—like there might be an end to it. Plus, and more important for Eloise, a certain amount of integration might serve to bridge the gap between her and David on one side and The Marriage on the other. At least it seemed possible.

Eloise was willing to listen. Still, she had a good idea what would come next.

"There will be a slight raise in my fees," said the counselor. "But the good news is that I will be providing additional services."

"Like what?" asked David.

"Well, I'm going to be supplying interface. Say, you want to get the marriage from A to B. Well, I interface between A and B."

"I'm not sure I get this," said David.

"Well, say you and Eloise resolve to be more candid with each other. I interface that. That way you get from less candid to more candid." The marriage counselor smiled, as if the smile itself would hasten comprehension.

Eloise tried to imagine what interfacing would look like. She pictured the marriage counselor's face between David and herself, but then nothing much happened.

"So what else do we get for this?" asked David.

"Well, you'll get the same services, plus some others. Probably the most important is that I will integrate your other consultants—your personal therapist, your personal trainer, nutritionist—anyone you have who has something to do with life planning and advice. I make sure that everything is streamlined. I try get rid of the kinks, the redundancies, and so on."

"I'm not sure we need that," said Eloise.

"Oh, Eloise, you'd be surprised. You too, David. Some of my clients have already told me, 'I don't know how I ever managed before.' Plus, after a few sessions . . . I won't need many with you," she said, patting Eloise on the thigh. "I will look into what sorts of things we can take out of your life and outsource."

"What—like grocery shopping?"

"Oh, everything and anything, Eloise. There's even this thing called emotional outsourcing I'm looking into."

"I don't know—this all sounds a bit too upscale for us."

"Well, it's your choice. You too, David. But that's what I'm going to do. I am now a Tier 1 consultant."

"What's that?" asked Eloise

"Well, basically it's what I've described. It involves oversight, integration, and facilitation."

Eloise caught a glimpse of David out of the corner of her eye. She could tell from the crease (as she called it) that things were not going well. The crease was a vertical line, roughly half an inch long, in the middle of David's forehead. Meteorologically speaking, it signaled impending bad weather. Not a hurricane, nor even a storm (David had neither the passion nor the wherewithal for truly angry behavior), but something akin to a Seattle overcast—a brooding, low, cloud cover. This wasn't so bad, but as in Seattle itself, the overcast could last weeks.

Eloise, who had been raised in a Brooklyn Jewish family known to yell at each other in good cheer at dinner, had been obliged to adjust her standards to discern the subtle signs emanating from David's WASP-y reserve: Seattle overcast was as bad as it ever got. The crease was as visible a symptom as there ever was.

And now, the crease was unmistakably there. Eloise really did want to know the meaning of "oversight, integration, and facilitation." She felt that the marriage counselor's earlier answers had been somewhat vague, overly general. But with the crease pending, Eloise decided her questions could wait.

"Eloise—and you too, David—you decide. I do have to tell you that in a couple of months, I will be doing this full-time. So if it's not something you want to do, I'll be able to help you with referrals."

■ ■ ■

The fight on the drive back home was not epic, but in fourteen years of marriage, it did rank in the top ten. It was the sort of fight that would be remembered long afterwards. Perhaps bitterly: "That is exactly like the time when you . . ." Or with bemusement: "Do you remember the time when we . . ." What was certain, however, is that it would be remembered.

"I am tired of going to a 'You-too-David' counselor," he said. "It's not helpful. I don't think it's counseling. I don't know what it is, but it's not helping me or the marriage either. That's two of us. You're outvoted."

"She's trying, David. And she gets us to talk."

"Like now?"

"Be fair."

"I am being fair. Just call me U2-David from now on. I think the principal problem with The Marriage *is* the marriage counselor."

"She's only trying to include you, David. It's your fault—you don't ever speak up."

"Fault? I thought we weren't supposed to do fault. Do you know how many times we have fought or argued over the counseling? I don't think we have any problems in this marriage besides the marriage counseling."

"Is it that she makes you feel bad?"

"Please, do not use that word with me."

"What word?"

"Feel. I think the feel word should be off-limits for at least a week—maybe a month. Right now, I am trying not to feel. I wish not to feel. And if by chance I do feel something, I don't want to talk about it."

"Oh David." Eloise sighed.

■ ■ ■

Eloise was not wholly unreceptive to David's problems with the marriage counselor. The past three years of processing had taken its toll. Now it seemed the counseling was reaching a crisis point, what with this Tier 1 thing.

Eloise was frankly uncertain about what to do. Complicating matters was that her own therapist seemed to have gone unaccountably AWOL. It was now virtually impossible to get an appointment. And whenever there was an opening, the assistant would invariably call a week or two later to cancel.

So therapy was out. That wouldn't have been so bad except that now, even shopping was losing some of its allure. And that was a serious matter—because, as Eloise well knew, shopping was core. Eloise was, by any fair account, an extremely accomplished shopper. Years in the aisles had taught her where the best deals would be found, when, and for what. Any attempt to reproduce her situated contextual knowledge from scratch would have required launching a small platoon of anthropologists on a field study of the L.A. mall scene. And even then, Eloise (being Eloise) would likely have had it all over them.

There were, of course, many kinds of shopping. For Eloise and her friends, shopping went through several phases. There was the shop-purchase-and-use phase. As their needs grew, there was the purchase-and-return phase. From there it was but a small, though morally questionable, slide into a purchase-use-and-return phase.

That last phase seemed to have possessed the entire group all at once when, on one Chardonnay-saturated evening by the pool, they all recalled their adolescent years, years marked by even more questionable shopping behaviors—most notably, the shoplift-never-return phase. And among the truly edgy (there were two of them), the nihilistic shoplift-and-trash phase.

Recalling the illicit joys of those heedless moments somehow prompted all members of the group to renew the interests of youth—which, given the onset of respectable middle age, they dialed down to a more appropriate formula, namely, purchase-use-and-return. It was a deliciously illicit moment in the lives of these women who had neither the gumption nor the spiritual corruption necessary to engage in higher order transgressions such as affairs or cocaine. For most of them (the two remained unchastened) purchase-use-and-return defined the outer bounds of risqué.

Everything went fine until one of them—it was Samantha, the youngest and most recent addition to the group—posed The Question. As Samantha put it—and in the annals of women's shopping, this was a moment at once universal, breakthrough, and utterly banal—"What's the point in shopping, in going from this store to that one, if you're not going to buy anything or you end up returning the stuff?"

This was a question that the male of the species has wanted to ask (and for the most part refrained from asking) since the dawn of the first Mesopotamian bazaar. Women, by contrast, had posed the question to themselves and each other with each new generation.

It was a good question, but it was not as if there were no answers. Eloise, for one, was prepared. She was smooth and succinct: "It's the process," she said.

"Uh, no, not so much," Samantha protested. "We spend all this time looking and going from mall to mall, looking for parking, but what's the point if we don't buy?"

Eloise sighed and, in a tone at once wise and weary, said, "It's the going that matters."

"Why? Like, I don't get that. What's the point in going, if you're not ever going to get there?"

Eloise wondered about this. For some reason, sex came to mind, confusion set in, and she had to let the argument drop. She thought there was something almost perverse in the way Samantha could derail her thinking. One moment they're talking about shopping, then it turns out to be about sex. How does that happen? Eloise could not figure it out.

In truth, it was not terribly complicated. It was, unfortunately for Eloise, her lot in life to be among women not any smarter than she but frequently much better educated. Women who knew things that she didn't. Samantha was one of those. A younger, hipper, and much better educated version of Eloise herself, Samantha had learned in grad school (virtually by osmosis) one of its primary lessons: anything can be about anything else. (And usually is.) Samantha had internalized this lesson as her way of being in the world, while Eloise had not even heard of the idea.

Eloise began to feel that she was losing grasp of things. Nothing seemed to be what it was supposed to be. It always seemed to be something else. Therapy was no longer therapy. Instead, it had become part of the problem. Even shopping had become complicated. Eloise felt unmoored. Things would have to change.

■ ■ ■

They did. It had nothing to do with David. Of this, Eloise was absolutely sure. What it did have to do with was quite unclear—to Eloise and to everyone else. But the facts themselves were uncontroverted.

When she walked into Soho's on 4th, she had not planned on buying gloves at all. Gloves were relatively useless in L.A. There was really no good time, no good occasion, to wear them. But upon noticing the white calfskin gloves on the display table next to the purses and the scarves, Eloise knew she wanted them. They felt so soft. The calfskin was deliciously liquid and the stitching so fine, one wondered whether they were stitched at all.

What happened next was never really in issue, but the why of it all—now *that* remained anyone's guess. Perhaps it was the recent recounting of the illicit shopping experiences of youth with her friends. Or perhaps it was because the salesperson left the room in such a hurry, leaving both Eloise and the gloves unattended. Or perhaps the gloves themselves were to blame. Whatever the reason, it happened that the gloves were suddenly picked up and stuffed deep into Eloise's purse. It was one swift, continuous gesture.

On one level Eloise could not believe she had done this. It was wrong. Impulsive. Risky. On a different level, it felt utterly thrilling. It was just a pair of gloves she had stolen, but for all the adrenalin coursing through her body, it might as well have been the crown jewels. All her senses were on high alert.

Everything went smoothly until she made her way down the first floor escalator. Almost as soon as she stepped on the stairs, she noticed the three men at the bottom. She wanted to turn around, but on an escalator, that was not really an option. She was going down. She thought that perhaps the three men would be gone by the time she arrived on the first floor. She looked down at them hopefully. They looked up, but not so hopefully.

Perhaps the three men would disperse. Perhaps they would be called away on more important business. Perhaps there would be an earthquake. Perhaps—Eloise was searching hard here—she had misinterpreted the situation. Guilt could do that. She knew. Eloise was now past the up escalator and in full view of the first floor. Anyone down there could look up and see her. Not that anyone had, but they could. The ordinariness of the scene below—the salespeople busy with their cash registers, the customers ambling down the aisles—that was a façade that could crack at any time. Any moment now the salespeople and customers—in Makeup, Foundations, Perfumes, Lingerie—would turn toward Eloise and say, "It's her. There she is."

The three men below were still there. Still looking up at her. Soon, eye contact would be made, and she would be called upon to smile in recognition—a perfunctory smile, the sort of nothing-smile that women issue mindlessly fifty, maybe a hundred times a day. The sort of smile that says and means nothing beyond, I acknowledge you as part of my species and I note that you are there. Surely she could pull that off. Maybe. She could have sworn that the escalator was actually slowing down.

When she stepped off, the three men blocked her way.

"May we please see your purse, ma'am?"

Those were the last words Eloise heard at Soho's on 4th that day because, at that precise moment, her body gently crumpled into itself like a compressed accordion. All of it, that is, except for her head, which struck a glass display table with a dull thud, like a baseball bat hitting a softball far into the outfield.

Eloise hit a home run: She was out for forty-five minutes.

■ ■ ■

She woke up in a bed not her own in a white room she had never seen before. She was hooked up to some machines by way of wires and tubes and other such medical paraphernalia. She was obviously in a hospital room, obviously in a hospital bed, and obviously a patient.

Next to her, sitting in a chair, reading a magazine, was David.

"How do you feel?" he asked.

"Woozy."

"The doctor said you might feel that way. It's the drugs."

"What happened?"

"You fainted."

"When can I go home?"

"Well, he's being pretty vague on that."

"Can you get me my purse?"

"They took back the gloves, hon. They were actually very nice about the whole thing. Why, Eloise?"

Eloise teared up. "I don't know," she said. "One moment the gloves were on the display table. And the next moment they were in my purse. And then it was too late. I'm so ashamed."

"Oh, it happens to everyone," said David, realizing instantaneously that no, probably it didn't. "It's not a big deal," he added quickly.

Eloise began to cry. She made small, wet sounds. Her eyes, nose, mouth, lips all stretched and pulled awkwardly in different directions—her face decomposing into separate features all doing their own thing as in a Picasso portrait. It was pitiful and not pretty, and it made David want to hug her. Which he did. "There, there . . . "

She rubbed her face and her eyes, which were red now. "I am tired David. I don't want to do this anymore," she said.

David was not entirely sure what "this" was, but he had some vague idea. And he had some idea what "tired" meant and why she would feel that way. He thought he understood. Because he was tired too. He too had broken down. Still, he wondered what breaking down had been like for her. That, he didn't know.

The Plan

"Come on people, think!" exclaimed Mariana. "We have a synopsis of the dissertation. You have J.T.'s newest article. Trish has gotten you all the stories that fit the pattern—Chicago, Philadelphia, D.C., Boston. And you have my memo on the conference at Berkeley. It's up to us to put it together."

"With David as our star? He's still a client, right?"

"He's a client. Maybe we'll use him, maybe we won't. I don't want to be tied down by the client thing at the beginning. Remember the KZLA interview thing was a complete bust. We'll see when we get the narrative straight. Now, who's got something?"

"Could we get Tony White?"

"We've got Tony White."

"No!"

Mariana smiled. "Let me tell you, it was not easy. The guy is pretty wary of publicists. I took him to a Lebanese restaurant after the conference. The guy would not let me pay!"

"How'd you get him?"

"He believes we're going to get his dissertation published."

"We own him, then?"

"Yep. He's ours. Let's get the narrative down, people."

"I'm thinking we need an event."

"Okay. Good. What kind of event?"

"Something big—national."

"National is good. Now, where would this event take place?"

"Well, it could be anywhere. The site really depends upon what sort of event."

"What about a survivor show?"

"Oh please. Come on people, think!"

"What if we have some sort of big public thing?"

"Okay. And?"

"Well, maybe we can just step back. What do these people want—the breakdowners?"

"Oooooh, I like that," said Mariana. "'The Breakdowners.' I don't know if you all read my memo on the conference. The academics couldn't figure it out. They were all over the place."

"Yeah, well, they're academics."

"What do the Breakdowners want?"

"To get from A to B."

"No. They want to stop having to go from A to B."

"Yeah, it's more like they want something else—something besides A to B."

"Basically, they don't want to be predictable."

"Okay. Stop." Mariana closed her eyes and drew a long deep breath. "Okay people, this is not working. Just give me one word. What do they want?"

"Meaning." The answer came from Julie, the intern, who was sitting at the far end of the conference table. The room fell silent. Everyone stared at Julie.

"Go on."

"They want meaning in their lives."

"And meaning would mean *what* precisely here?"

"No, no, wait, she's got a real idea here," said Mariana, holding up her hands to quiet everyone. "Meaning," she said. "We can work with that."

"What kind of meaning?"

"You know, meaning in general."

"What meaning is that?"

"It doesn't matter. That's the beauty of the thing," said Mariana. "All we need is for meaning to be revealed—"

"—at an event."

"*The* Event!"

"Exactly."

"Now, what we need is a site—*The* Site."

"The rest will take care of itself."

"Do David and Tony still fit in?"

"I think they'll both resonante with the meaning thing. Tony is big on seeing. He wants to *see*."

"I'm not comfortable with the meaning thing. I'm not sure it'll take care of itself—even if we have a great event or a great site."

"Oh, really?"

"Yeah, really. Suppose we have an event and a site. What guarantee do we have that meaning will come out of it?"

"Uh . . . press, media, politicians, pundits, producers, experts, talking heads—need I go on?" said Mariana. "Want to think again?"

"But Mariana, where's our narrative? You always want narrative."

"Alright. Fair enough. We'll have someone working on the meaning thing."

"Do we do workups on Tony and David?"

"David we've already got. Tony can wait. Okay. So who wants to work on the meaning thing? No, wait. We're going to have an integrated team: Event-Site-Meaning—ESM. I need three volunteers."

Julie, the intern, raised her hand.

"Thank you, Julie, but we really need staff to do this."

"No, I just had a question. If we have an event, how do we make money off David and Tony? I mean, how does that work?"

Everyone chuckled.

"We own them, Julie. Anything they want to write, shoot, sell, market, distribute, publicize, promote, recant—anything at all, we own ten percent of that."

"Yes, but what do they have to market?"

Mariana held up an index finger and smiled. "Julie, that's

where we come in. We make sure they're part of The Event, and that's what we'll call it: The Event. We write them into the script, the show, whatever. It doesn't really matter what happens, so long as they're part of it. That's our job. Everything is as it happens: the client, The Event, The Site, The Meaning. Everything except legal. Legal we do beforehand. And if David and Tony bail or screw up, we'll just get another client. Worse comes to worst, we'll create one. I'll notify legal. Are we all on the same page now? Okay. Now remember, at 2:00, we have that group interview with our candidate—the psych Ph.D. Harvard? Or is it Princeton? Design and marketing. Play up our rankings, people. I think we're going to go up by the time she has to decide on her offers. That's if she works out for us. This is not a done deal. Be there! Ciao. Oh, wait—one more thing. Who rented her car while she's here?"

"Me. An Audi TT, convertible, Aruba blue pearl exterior, limestone gray Alcantera leather. Six-speed, S Tronic transmission."

"Moonroof?"

"Not available."

"Damn," said Mariana as she closed her laptop.

Mariana went back to her office. She leaned back in her jet black Italian leather chair. Uncharacteristically, she became pensive. Probably it was because she did not like lying to her staff. Still, lying was sometimes necessary, and this definitely had been one of those times. The truth of the matter was that Tony White was not a client. He'd never been a client. Tony had refused to sign. Mariana would have to depend upon David (and, given his last performance, that was not an auspicious prospect), or she would have to find someone else. Event, Site, Meaning—it was all still quite nebulous.

"C"

The idea became known as "C." It supposedly came from Tony White, though no one really knew. The idea had been picked up by the blogs, talk radio, and some local morning news shows. When news of C broke in the serious national media, Jon Stewart on *The Daily Show* had a field day. He couldn't get enough. With almost any guest on his show—it didn't matter who: an undersecretary at the State Department, Bon Jovi, the British ambassador—Stewart would invariably ask, "So! Enough chit chat. What about this C thing? Can you give us an update on C?" At first, the question drew blanks among the guests. But as C circulated (and it did) the whole idea gained a certain substance—a thing to talk about and analyze. A topic for prognostication.

Of course, no one actually knew what C meant. But conceptually, the idea was enticingly clear: If going from A to B had become passé or tiresome, if it was leading to breakdowns, then why not an extension? Not so much a sequel, or even an incremental addition, and certainly not the usual recycling. Instead, something at once totally expected and yet totally not. Hence, C. A, B, C. Only C (and here the media played an indispensable role) was to be of a completely different order of magnitude. C was often referred to in the media and elsewhere as something that would be revealed at "The Event." The Event, in turn, would take place at something called "The Site." At first, The Site was GPS-indeterminate. It was a nebulous, apparently geographically transient concept. Venues ranged from San Francisco to Burning Man in Nevada to Seattle and the Hamptons. Gradually, determinacy took hold, and The Site (once an abstract concept) settled on Arco, Idaho, located some sixty miles west of Idaho Falls on U.S. Route 26. (The actual site was in the desert almost eight miles from Arco, but everyone settled on Arco as the name.)

"Why Arco?" people asked. Again, no one knew. It was a small town (population around 2,000), and there was lots of space all around. Much of it starkly beautiful. But that didn't really answer the question. For a while the theory was bandied about that it was because Arco was the first city to get its electricity from nuclear power (1955). Yet when people asked why that would matter, the theory sort of foundered. Ultimately, the press settled on a common story line. It was the contrarian aspect, they said: Who would have thought of Arco? And that, as they argued, that was precisely the point: Who, after all, would have thought of Woodstock?

As an op-ed in the *Washington Post* noted, Remus and Romulus founded Rome, and they were wolves—so why not a gathering at Arco? History is devious. It has its ways.

Somehow a date had to be found. Internet polling did its magic. The date was set: June 15.

The Multipliers

June 15 was months away. Meanwhile excitement grew. Tony White's doctoral dissertation was located and posted and reposted and downloaded endlessly, as were two of his articles (one on late period Abyssinian poetry and the other a puzzling disquisition on French surrealism).

As for Tony himself, he had to confine his whereabouts within the metes and bounds of the commune or else face unscrupulous inquiries from a rapacious and predatory press. Even though Tony showed no signs of leaving, there was always one or another white news van lying in wait at the bottom of the dirt driveway. Occasionally, Tony would wave at them. They waved back.

Soon The Event crossed some invisible tipping point in national media consciousness. Social media went crazy. CNN actually had a daily news segment called "The Event Watch." Soon even the running daily commentary on the Christian Fairfax case (a cheating husband with a sneering smile who had allegedly dismembered his wife) was displaced by The Event. There were, of course, all sorts of speculations as to what The Event would be, whether it would be a success, a turning point, a milestone for the country, or something as yet unimagined. The spirituality index made huge gains, rapture made a comeback (it would happen on June 15—this time they were sure), and conspiracy theories multiplied at exponential rates. Top internet searches included:

June 15 + "Trilateral Commission"
June 15 + "Protocols of the Elders of Zion"
June 15 + socialism
June 15 + "Federal Reserve"

And, of course, since everything eventually turns meta:

June 15 + conspiracy

As discussion filtered and congregated, amassed and disseminated, cyber hierarchies emerged. As chance would have it, one of the earliest Tony White websites (there were literally dozens) seemed to garner the most attention: http://artichoke.whatev.org, a state of the art website devoted to everything about Tony White. They adopted the artichoke as their symbol. They posted all sorts of materials, including Tony's dissertation, photographs of Tony (some arguably photoshopped), a song written by Tony they found on YouTube, and several hot and cold artichoke dish recipes.

The one thing that was off-limits on the site was "C." There was to be no discussion of "C"—not in the postings nor in the comments. The webmaster was draconian. This self-censorship turned out to be something of a mistake because a lot of the traffic drifted over to another website: http://c.whatev.org.

Soon http://c.whatev.org became the primary site for cascades of speculations, ruminations, and predictions about C. What C could be, whether it would work, and so on. There were even "how-to" postings on how to get to C. Never mind that, as many pointed out, C wouldn't arrive until The Event, which in turn wouldn't happen until June 15. But this was America, the land of rugged individualism where surely, if there was a communal way to get somewhere, there had to be a way to get there all by one's self. And so it was that there were numerous articles on how to get beyond TATBTNGA (still pronounced "Tab Naga") and reach C.

The most popular of the Getting Beyond Tab Naga techniques (or "GBs" for short) was to engage in a purposeless activity. The theory (one with clear theological pedigrees) being that if one embraced the "great emptiness" of it all, there would be a great resulting vacuum, thus enticing C to arrive. As with its theological predecessors, it was not generally noticed that a "great emptiness" could serve as hospitable psychic ground for the reception, not just of C, but of anything at all (including alien possession or IRS audits). Be that as it may, it was at first thought that meditation, deep breathing, treadmills, and tanning salons (all of which had their champions) qualified as purposeless activities. This worked well enough until it was pointed out that all these activities had side benefits and thus couldn't be considered entirely purposeless.

Second generation GBs came out within a matter of weeks. "GB Sisyphus" (a free download) became a popular game—particularly among sultry, post-adolescent males—who for some reason found it inspiring to push an imaginary cyber-boulder up an imaginary cyber-hill only to watch it cyber-fall down again. GB Sisyphus was a one-level game, had no scoring option, no obvious end to it, and was available only in earth tones reminiscent of the Seattle grunge era. One post pointed out that but for the absence of lights, bonus rounds, and scoring, GB Sisyphus was the distilled essence of pinball. Where one was supposed to go with that was left unclear, but after all, it was just a post. A more cynical blogger pointed out that GB Sisyphus was not at all a way to get beyond A to B, but on the contrary, it was doing the A-to-B thing with a vengeance. Indeed, GB Sisyphus was nothing but going from A to B. If this was not obvious on first impression, it's only because the players were inevitably failing at it, as the cyber-boulder always fell back down to A. "This," added the poster, "is what comes of too much huffing," leading the next poster to ask just how much huffing would be just right. And so it went, following the seemingly inexorable multiplier logic of posting and counter-posting and interro-posting, and RSS aggregation and meta-RSS aggregation, and, of course, the usual viral and phishing permutations.

On the whole, peak interest was reached rather quickly. Some of the news networks returned to daily coverage of the Christian Fairfax case, where it was discovered that the cheating husband (still out on bail) was once a cocaine abuser and French.

In short, all this blogging and posting and social media seemed to confirm what the most savvy already knew: There would be no C before The Event happened. Period.

The Pilgrimage

According to Mariana, David had been invited to open the ceremonies for The Event on Friday evening, and Mariana was pushing him hard to accept. David didn't want to. For one thing, he really didn't have much to say. He recalled the conference. And while it had been interesting, he recalled that he really didn't have much to say there either. His interest, like everyone else, was C. He wanted to be there when C happened. Besides, things had moved on: The A-to-B stuff, the Madden Act, the Breakdowners in New York, Chicago, Boston—that was old news. C was the thing now. That's pretty much all anybody talked about. Mariana continued to press David nonetheless, saying that this was his chance to make a difference—"Really make a difference, David." She said there would be lots of people at Arco—people like him, tired of going from A to B and wanting something different, something more. "It's our turn to give, David," she said. "Be a giver, David," she said. David was not convinced.

Plus he didn't want to go if it would upset Eloise. She steadfastly maintained she was indifferent, though David knew very well she was testing him. It was obvious she wanted him to stay! There was Emily's graduation from fourth grade and a longstanding dinner party with the Bernsteins next door.

In the end, Mariana gave up on trying to persuade David. Instead, she lured Eloise: "I think it would be good for David," she told Eloise. "He needs to get out of himself. And this will open up his possibilities. You could go with him." And so not only did David go, but he brought Eloise and Emily, along. Off they went: East on the 10, then North on 15 towards Las Vegas and Salt Lake City, and on to Arco.

■ ■ ■

As for Mariana, she booked herself and her team first class seats on a direct flight to Boise. From there a rental limo would take them to Arco, and from there to The Site. She reminded everyone to bring bathing suits because there were hot springs everywhere and that she preferred not to see her staff naked.

■ ■ ■

Michael Zelnack had originally planned to walk to Arco. His idea was to retrace Jack Kerouac's route, but to do it on foot. He could make it as far as Laramie and maybe cut off through the Wind

River. At this point, walking full-time everyday, Michael was a lean, mean, walking machine. He'd lost some fifteen pounds, which was pretty amazing given the muscle he'd put on. Still, after consulting the maps, he realized that walking to Arco would take at least four months. And so he decided to hitch—which was more in keeping with his impromptu paean to Jack Kerouac anyway.

Like everybody else, Michael wanted to learn about C. Occasionally, in his more optimistic moments, he even thought there might be a chance that C could help him jump-start his book. Perhaps the book itself might be about C. The possibilities were wide open.

The Site

The general public started trickling into Arco on Monday. By Tuesday, the whole area was a carnival. The Idaho State Police then blocked U.S. Route 26 from the East and the South, and U.S. Route 93 from the North. There were reports of a few skirmishes at the blockades. Words were exchanged. Punches thrown. Arrests made. But all in all, given the immense size of the gathering and the frustrations of traffic, the pilgrims were remarkably peaceful. One thing was for sure: No one was deterred by the police presence. No one turned around. The upshot was that U.S. Route 26 was gridlocked from Interstate 84 on the south to well past Idaho Falls to the east.

Meanwhile, the SUVs, the pickups, the Jeeps, the Chevys, the

Mercedes, and the BMWs drove on to Arco cross-country, right through the desert, ripping through sage and kicking up an awful lot of dust. On Wednesday, the governor reversed his prior decision and allowed the gathering to take place. The Idaho National Guard was called out to monitor traffic, provide security, and assist with first aid, food, water, and sanitation. Homeland Security hovered on the perimeter. Dr. Miloh Cedar, head of the agency, explained that The Idaho National Laboratory, a nuclear research facility (coincidentally, also called "The Site") was only twenty miles away. In such circumstances, Homeland Security could not afford to take any chances.

By Thursday, more than two million people had descended on Arco, waiting peacefully for The Event to begin.

Drugs flowed freely, though actually few partook. Pot, X, coke—only a little meth. There was some bad heroin on Thursday, and a dozen people ended up in the makeshift infirmary. The bands succeeded each other without a hitch—metal, country, indie, alternative, folk. Some participants had come prepared with barbecues, coolers, beers, and hot dogs. Others were totally unprepared. Food had to be shipped in by helicopter: sandwiches and pizza mostly. Gourmet food it was not, but it tasted pretty good, and no one complained. People lit bonfires at night, but these were invariably extinguished by "The Guard," as it came to be called. Except for this single isolated kill-joy function, The Guard achieved high marks for its professionalism and courtesy.

All this was a prelude to "C." No one knew exactly what

would come, though rumors circulated widely. Some believed that Tony White would make an appearance. Others held out for something more apocalyptic. Something transcendent. Spiritual. Transformative.

On Friday morning, Michael Baxter, the Republican senator from Idaho, came to talk to the crowd. He spoke of the American Dream, the frontier spirit, and taxes being too high. After a few minutes, people lost interest and started chanting, "Bring back the music. We want music!"

One young woman in a sarong interviewed on KBF Idaho summed up The Event. "It's the Woodstock of our generation. It totally rocks," she said. "All these people have come here from all parts of the country to be as one. We don't care that it all started in L.A. We're beyond that. This is The Event, we're at The Site, and we're all waiting for C. This is all about peace and love. And getting really high. They say Muse is going to play." A man interviewed by CNN explained, "It's about control. We're trying to get our lives back. We have come here to reclaim the American Dream. To stand up and be counted." A grandmother from Nebraska chimed in, "The Event is about getting the government off our backs." An elderly man from Oregon was more contemplative. "I've been through a lot, man. Never had any use for this A-to-B shit. Lived in the Haight back in the day when the Dead played for five dollars down at the Fillmore. Went to Nam. Dropped acid. Dropped my old lady. Dropped out of med school. The reason I'm here, you know, is to see what's going on. That's why I'm here—to see.

Cause, it's like, if you don't see what's going on, well then really, what's the fuckin' point? I mean, what else is there?"

These were some of the more colorful characters. And while they got more than their share of airtime on the talk shows and the networks, they were not representative. On the contrary, most of those present were ordinary suburban and exurban families—from New Jersey, California, Utah. The kids played frisbee and soccer and chased each other around the R.V.'s. In the evening, the grown-ups sat around the campfires, sunburned and dusty, but happy to be in each other's company as they waited for C to happen. Only a very few had been to Woodstock. But now they had all been to Arco—which must have been much the same, only family style.

■ ■ ■

By Friday evening, it was pretty clear to the assembled crowd that C would arrive some time Saturday. Saturday came, hot and dusty, but the people waited patiently. There were announcements and more bands. At one point, a long-haired man took the stage and announced that the moment had come. He talked about peace and "overriding bliss" and "climbing the mountain" in order to get to it. He pointed off in the distance towards the Sawtooth Range. And he said, "There be the Mountain. There be the bliss." Then he started yelling, "I am C! I am C!" and jumping up and down like a madman (which, apparently, he was). After a while, two Guardsmen climbed the stage and gently ushered him away.

The kids, who by now had grown tired of playing soccer, invented a game they called "Meaning Hunt." The idea was to lift up big rocks one at a time. The first person who lifted a rock, revealing another rock underneath, was the winner. The winner got to hold the "meaning rock" and say what he or she thought C would be (when C arrived). Then they'd do it again. As the ages of the children varied considerably, so did the meanings ascribed to C. It was suggested that C would likely be "a spaceship," "a big dragon with fire coming out of his mouth," "Lady Gaga," "a truck full of ice cream," and "my birthday."

The meaning hunts went on for a couple hours on Saturday afternoon until the Guard put an end to them when three kids, instead of finding meaning under the rocks, uncovered a couple of gopher snakes. They were not poisonous, but they did scare the kids something fierce, and it gave everyone pause. The announcement on the loudspeaker was gentle but firm: "This is Sergeant McTavor of the Idaho National Guard. Meaning is not found under rocks. This is desert country, people, and we do have rattlesnakes out here. So please make sure your children don't lift any more rocks. Thank you, and have a great day."

■ ■ ■

For the first time in a very (very) long time, Mariana was nervous. She had lost David, who, after numerous entreaties, simply declined to take any active part in The Event. He was there, of course, but he would not speak. It was fine to own all the rights to David (who was contractually unbundled and partitioned to within an inch of his life), but if he didn't do anything, there wouldn't be a whole lot to sell, promote, market, parlay, leverage, license, or whatever. Tony White, who had never signed on, was apparently so dubious about The Event that he decided not to attend. Soon Mariana would have to tell her staff another lie about Tony. *Like what?* she wondered. She had lost him as a client? Like that was believable.

This left Mariana, a premier publicist, with a novel predicament, at least for her: She did not have a client who could be counted on to perform. The best she could do was operate after the fact—get someone to sign after they'd done whatever it was they did. That was not hopeless, but it was uncertain, and definitely not the sort of work situation she imagined for herself. She had to hope that someone would do something interesting and that she could get to them first.

It was all a bit galling to her that The Event and The Site and C were, in a manner of speaking, the creations of her agency, Incandescence, Inc., and that now she controlled none of them. The fact that her agency used those terms merely as empty placeholders to be filled in by others is something she did not bring to mind. It was all form anyway. And usually, in Mariana's professional life, form was perfectly adequate to produce its own content.

As she surveyed the vast mass of humanity surrounding her—their automotive vehicles, their barbecues, their royal blue canvas soccer chairs, their coolers, their boom boxes, and their American flags—she finally asked herself the questions she had conveniently bracketed all this time: How am I going to find meaning here? Where is *my* C? What does he, or she, or it look like?

■ ■ ■

Inasmuch as Tony White had made abundantly clear to Mariana that he was not going to attend The Event, there seemed to be little chance that he would change his mind. But on Sunday, without any evidence of C in sight, the crowd had become a bit more agitated. At various times on Sunday morning, they broke into full-throated cries of, "Toe-nee, Toe-nee, Toe-nee." And at other times, they chanted, "We are here. We are here. Where are you? Where are you?"

Tony was apprised of all this both by Jennifer Olivetti, a cable news anchor, and by a Brigadier General of the National Guard. The Brigadier General, who did not want to face the collective disenchantment of 2.5 million people, was keen on producing some happy conclusion. If C were to come along, a lot of his problems would be resolved. More important perhaps is that some rather nasty new ones—crowd control came to mind—would not arise. If this Tony White could be persuaded to come to The Site and serve as C, then that was all to the best. The Brigadier General was a relatively recent graduate of West Point, so the idea that military operations should be a function of media spin was neither novel nor strange to him. And if this Jennifer Olivetti person could help in this worthy endeavor, then so much the better. The Brigadier

General, of course, had not the slightest illusion about Jennifer's sense of social responsibility. On the contrary, he saw her for what she was—a positively reptilian careerist. But here their interests seemed to converge. As the Brigadier General told some of the assembled officers at a working breakfast earlier, "2.5 million people is nothing to fuck around with."

And so at the last minute, as a result of long phone calls from the Brigadier General and Jennifer Olivetti, Tony decided to go to Arco. The late offer of a helicopter from Jennifer Olivetti was accepted. Still he cautioned her, "I'll go, but I'm not sure I want to say anything." The helicopter had been waiting for him in Idaho Falls for the last three hours. Interstates 84 and 86 were still totally blocked—a long strip line of cars stretching like a loose belt around Idaho's oversized southern regions.

Things looked promising for Jennifer Olivetti. But then, talking with him on the helicopter on the way out, she overdid it. "We'd like you to talk up meaning," she told Tony.

"I have no idea what you're talking about."

"We want you to—"

"Who is this 'we'? Don't you just cover the news?"

Jennifer chuckled, "We make the news. Covering the news is not something we do unless we absolutely have to."

"Well, so talking up this meaning thing—what do you have in mind?"

"Well, the people want meaning, and we want you to give it to them."

"I don't know how to do that. I have enough trouble just on my own." He looked west toward the mountain range appearing on the horizon. He shook his head and tried to pop his ears. "Is that where we're going?" he asked, pointing with a nod of his head.

"Somewhere in there. Chewing gum?" Jennifer asked, holding out a pack.

Tony took a piece and asked, "Well, what do they want?"

"They want a leader, a wise man. Surely you can give them something."

"Like what?"

"I don't know. You're the leader of a commune, aren't you?"

"We grow artichokes."

"But you're still their leader!"

"Yes. And that means I decide on what day we start harvesting. And only after we all talk about it—usually for hours."

At that point, they arrived in the vicinity of Arco. Tony could see a large area covered with people and obscured by dust. They were close to The Site. The setting sun gave the entire area an eerie, sepia orange glow.

The helicopter made a couple of runs over the crowd. Because of the noise of the engines and the blades, he could only barely make out the roar of the crowd. Still, he heard their chant: "What do we want?" "Meaning!" "When do we want it?" "Now!" "What do we want?" "Meaning!" "When do we want it?" "Now!"

That clinched it for Tony. *I should have known better,* he thought.

"I can't do it," he said.

Jennifer Olivetti was shocked. "You can't back out," she said. "They're expecting you. You're their hero. They think you're C. If you don't go down, all hell will break loose. I can get the Brigadier General to confirm it. I'm sure."

"I don't want to talk to the Brigadier General."

The crowd began a new chant: "C . . . C . . . C . . . C"—this one in 4/4 time.

"Tony, I don't think you want this on your conscience."

"What do you care? If all hell breaks loose, it'll up your audience ratings."

Jennifer bit her lip. She hadn't considered this angle. Neither had home base in Houston, apparently. Was Houston slipping, or was she?

It didn't matter. The fact is that now, stuck at a five hundred feet in the air with this infernal mind-sapping helicopter noise, she would have to make a command decision.

The command decision she made was to call home base. She leaned toward the pilot, nestling her hand on his arm. "I can't get reception on my cell. Can you patch me through to my network in Houston?"

"Sure thing, miss."

"Houston, this is Jennifer Olivetti. We're at the site. Mr. Tony White doesn't want to land. I'm thinking that if he doesn't, it may be very upsetting for the crowd . . . Incredibly loud . . . Possible riot . . . Within sight of the landing platform . . . They think he's

C. I'm pretty sure . . . How do you want to play this? Yes. Okay. Right. Right."

Jennifer turned to the pilot. "We're going home."

"No," said Tony. "Take me down."

The Event

From the back of the stage, out of the darkness, Tony walked up to the microphone. As soon as he stepped into the floodlights, the crowd began cheering and hollering—all of it at once and all of it really (really) loud. Dust rose from the desert floor. The scaffolding shook, and the stage shimmied. Gradually the noise morphed into a steady chant of "Toe-nee, Toe-nee, Toe-nee." Tony waved his arms downward to quiet the crowd, but the volume only increased, so he stopped. After five minutes of solid noise, the crowd finally settled, allowing Tony to speak.

"This is a great moment," he said, and once again the crowd broke into deafening cheers. "You have all come here, from all parts of the nation, to express a need for something more in your lives. Some of you came here tired of the A-to-B-thing-and-never-getting-anywhere. Others came here because you can't seem to get beyond A. And still others have come here because you feel like you're simply going around in circles.

"You have heard from all sorts of experts and pundits as to what the problem is and how to resolve it. I'm here to tell you that the power is in you."

Again the crowd erupted into cheers, though less loudly.

"That doesn't mean it's going to be easy. It's not. I want to talk to you about something that's tough to talk about."

Some people shuffled their feet. Others leaned forward in anticipation.

"I want to talk to you about life and death."

The crowd murmured. The D-word is not what they expected from C.

"The average life expectancy for an American today is roughly 78 years. In the history of humankind that is a blip. In the history of the universe, it is a micro-blip. But for each of us, it is not a blip at all. For each of us, it's huge. We didn't get to choose when our blip would be. But we're here now, and the question is, what are we going to do with our blip?

"Most people in America just go along with whatever happens to be going on," Tony continued. "They don't ask the question, and so they do what they're expected to do. And what they're expected to do is set by the advertisers, the pundits, the media, the corporations, the politicians, the priests, the teachers, and so on."

Tony took a couple large gulps of water. "And so . . . and so they don't ever ask, what am I going to do with these seventy-some-odd years? They just live the stories that the culture fashions for them. Now, I'm not saying that we should try to live outside our times. But I do think we should choose how to live—as opposed to simply doing what we've been told. The big problem—and this explains why we are all here—is that the narratives our culture channels us into are increasingly meaningless. You have said so in so many ways.

"This is the problem with *our* blip. It's hardly the worst blip-problem to have. We could have been born during the dark ages. It's important to remember that. But it doesn't resolve our problem.

"And the question is: what are we going to do with our blip?

"My answer is to see. Now, people have asked me, 'See what?'"

The crowd took up a new chant: "C-what? C-what? C-what?"

"They ask me and I say: life is absurd."

Many in the crowd looked at each other. Almost all came to Arco not sure what C would be. But it's fair to say that, for the vast majority, absurdity was not the C they had in mind.

"Why is it so important to recognize that life is absurd? Why?"

"Why? Why? Why?" echoed the crowd.

Tony smiled, as he was getting used to the crowd's rhythms. "The reason is simple. Until you see how absurd human life actually is, you cannot really take charge of it as your own. You cannot make it your own or decide how to live your blip. Why is that?"

Tony paused for emphasis.

"Why? It's because so many of our institutions are themselves absurd. And so you get caught up in *their* absurdities—many of which are silly and shallow. You end up wasting *your* blip working on *their* absurdities. So my message to you is—look absurdity in the face. And then recognize just how amazing it is that you have been given this blip. It's huge."

"Huge! Huge! Huge!" they chanted.

"That's it," he said. "Thank you."

The crowd stood up and cheered. Still, many wondered just what it was that had just happened. It was on their faces—expressions of surprise, traces of bewilderment: This was C? Life is absurd? Life is a blip? This was why they had traveled hundreds of miles to the Southern Idaho desert—to learn that life was an absurd blip?

Some of the reactions were swift and decisive.

"Man, that really sucks."

"Whoa! Dude—blew me away. Who would have thought!"

"No honey, Mommy's sure—life is not absurd."

The Meaning

The interviews started immediately. The reporters mingled in the crowd like announcers after a Super Bowl game. Microphones were thrust in faces. Questions asked. Interviewees prodded.

A young woman from Oregon in a blue shell jacket said, "It was amazing. It's as close to the truth as we've ever been told. The guy is a hero. People don't think about hard things, and so they end up missing out. He's just right on. The question is, what will people do with this?" As to what she would do, the young woman already had a pretty good idea. She would wind her way to Tony's commune in the Russian River valley.

Not all reactions were so sanguine. One man wearing an Atlanta Braves baseball cap interviewed on "American Patriot" said, "Yeah, he wants all of us to be absurd. He just came straight out in favor of absurdity. I don't think that's what this country was built on." The man was articulate and pleasant to look at in a beefy-hefty American sort of way. Later he would become a frequent guest on "American Patriot"—a sort of hands-on expert on Tony White.

One local Idaho radio station from Boise interviewed a group of children. The reactions were generally mixed, although common ground emerged early with the first boy interviewed: "Tony said we don't have to do homework." This view was later elaborated into a considerably more sweeping theoretical stance: "Yeah, we don't have to do anything." The other responses were more eclectic: "Is Ab-zurd like recess?"

Among the crowd, a sizeable and disappointed contingent felt that Tony and his speech could not possibly be C at all. Some of them stayed on in Arco after Tony left, convinced that C had yet to come—that if only they waited patiently, C would eventually arrive. Every night, they would gather around the stage (their numbers dwindling gradually) and recite an old chant, albeit in a newly mournful tone, "We are here. We are here. Where are you? Where are you?"

■ ■ ■

Among those who stayed to await C after Tony's speech, most eventually trickled away back to Saginaw, or Newton, or Cripple Creek, or wherever it was they called home. But some became so enamored of the Idaho desert and the Sawtooth Range that they decided to settle in the area. The immediate effect was to quadruple the population of Arco and to dramatically increase property values as well as the welfare rolls. It turned out that most who stayed behind were either very wealthy or destitute.

One of those who stayed was Michael Zelnack, who had arrived in Arco right in the middle of Tony's speech. Michael was seduced by the striking beauty of the area—the harshness of the desert with its orange, purple, and olive hues, the violence of the mountains with their jagged edges, the desolate comfort of the ceaseless streams and brooks. For Michael, who had never truly seen the West (L.A. and San Francisco didn't count), this inaugural encounter had the force of revelation: What better place to confront the absurdity of the American condition? Indeed, what else was there to think about out here?

Michael became convinced that if there were such a thing as the Great American Novel—something he sincerely doubted—it would have to be written from a place like Arco. A place barely this side of civilization, painfully eked out against the elements in the middle of nowhere, and at the junction of nothing. Here was a landscape to match the grand, sweeping emptiness at the heart of the American dream—a portal into the restlessness that animated the American soul. And a natural scenery so excruciatingly beautiful, it had to hold the promise of redemption.

He would stay.

First thing he did was buy a pickup—a 1989 Chevy.

Second thing he did was get a job as a night-time gas station attendant.

Third thing he did was pick a title for his book. (He would not share it with anyone.)

Michael was one for whom Tony's message of absurdity resonated deeply. Indeed, not only was Michael intimately familiar with the vagaries of the New York publishing industry (a veritable petri dish of absurdity), but he had, all on his own, come to think that the two-book system was absurd. In fact, "absurd" was exactly the word he used—even before coming out to Arco.

As Michael saw it, there were different layers of absurdity, ranging from the most pedestrian and unreflective to the most profound and articulate. The New York publishing industry was a low-level absurdity, sustained only because people went along with it. Driving around like the L.A. drivers—that was a kind of mid-level absurdity. It intimated a sense of irony. But the truest, most accomplished absurdity—that would be found here, in a place like Arco, among the courageous but doomed efforts of human beings to carve out an existence from an unforgiving landscape fated to reclaim sooner or later what was its own.

Not only would Arco allow Michael a full-on confrontation with the heart and soul of absurdity, but what more auspicious place than this barren landscape to yield a true, lasting meaning capable of enduring the harshest conditions? If one could create meaning here, then surely one could create it anywhere. Or so Michael thought.

The fact that he was deeply mistaken on both counts (barrenness had no particularly intimate connection to either meaning or absurdity) did not prevent him, as things turned out, from writing a first-rate novel. It was a serious novel—one that subtly led the reader to ponder whether the principle of his or her being lay in "earth" (the drive to return, seek refuge, and tap into the primal foundations) or "sky" (the urge to escape, flee, and start over). Earth or Sky. Security or Freedom. East or West. It took a while to write the book (the "suffering is time" theory), but when it came out, the reviews were rave. "Michael Zelnack's *The Two-book System*," wrote the reviewer for the *NY Times Book Review*, "may not be the Great American Novel, but it definitively puts to rest the idea that there are only two books to be written."

■ ■ ■

Among the most enthusiastic fans of Tony's performance, few were more ecstatic than Mariana. "The man is a frigging rock star!" she told Trish, her assistant. "We have to get in touch with him right away. We need to get bookings right now. Call his cell!"

"But you told us at Arco that he wasn't our client anymore—that he reneged."

"Well, we'll just have to try again."

As for Tony, he was not a fan of his own performance. As the helicopter whisked him away into the west that night, he tried to collect his thoughts. He wished that he had heeded his initial instincts: Don't go. Turn around. Don't do it.

As the helicopter made its way in the darkness towards Idaho Falls, Tony punished himself for failing to appreciate the full absurdity of his effort. He had forced it. The absurd was like anything else in life: It had its moments. But the idea of transforming the recognition of absurdity into a mantra was itself utterly absurd (or not nearly absurd enough). It was, in any event, a profoundly mistaken enterprise.

Absurdity was not everything. It was only something. And even then, only sometimes.

"We have to talk," Mariana exclaimed over the phone. "In person, as soon as possible. Where are you?"

"I don't know. High over Interstate 84 on the way to Boise."

"Where are you staying? I'll come to you."

"I don't know that we have anything to talk about."

"Oh, yes we do! Are you staying in Boise?"

"I'm going straight home. If you want, come to Russian River."

"I'll be waiting for you," she said.

And she was. Waiting. She stopped the rental car at an organic bakery to ask for directions to the artichoke commune. The sales girl smiled coyly and wrote down instructions.

When Mariana arrived, she saw a big, old, dilapidated ranch house and a huge barn. The latter had a relatively recent coat of red paint and inspired more confidence than the house. Below were the rows of artichoke plants, running parallel to each other off toward the ocean. Not doing too well, either.

There was a breeze pushing thin wisps of fog inland. Mariana was tired after having been up all night, but she found the beads of moisture on her face soothing—invigorating even.

A young man approached. "Can I help you?"

"I'm a publicist. Is Tony here yet?"

"No. He went to Arco."

"I know. He's on his way back. Is there anywhere I can sit?"

The young man pointed to a bench on the porch.

"We have lunch at 11:30. We get up early here," he said.

"Isn't the climate too cold and overcast for artichokes up here?" asked Mariana.

"Definitely."

"Then why artichokes?"

"Yeah. It's kind of silly, isn't it?"

Tony didn't make it back to the commune until late afternoon. That evening, Mariana laid out for Tony her plans for him: a press conference, the talk shows, the news circuit, a website, guest articles on various blogs, another interview with *The New Amsterdam*.

Tony was not into it. "Nope. Not doing it," he said.

"Will you at least do a book?"

Tony considered this briefly. "Tell you what—you come out here and work on the commune for a month, and I'll consider doing your book if you still want me to."

"I couldn't possibly! I have clients. My business!"

"Well, have that Julie what's-her-name take care of them."

"She's an intern!"

"You have other employees. Look, I don't really care, it's up to you."

Mariana was surprised to find herself actually thinking about it. When she went to bed that night, she couldn't sleep. One month of her life versus the client of a lifetime. By morning, she had made her decision: She wanted the challenge. What's the worst that could happen?

The Wind Down

As it turned out, Mariana was far from the only young woman to find her way to the artichoke commune. The woman in the blue shell jacket interviewed in Arco also drove there. And in fact there were numerous other young women, all quite taken by Tony White's message (or Tony White himself), who made the pilgrimage to the Russian River.

The first to arrive were heartily welcomed into the commune. But as more trickled in, the numbers became unmanageable, and the commune grudgingly turned them away.

The commune rejects were disappointed. Some resolved to build their own artichoke commune, thinking that artichokes were "The Way."

As for the internet, it was abuzz with interpretations and endorsements, as well as rejections of Tony's message. The traffic on http://artichokers.whatev.org, which had been declining before The Event, revived instantly. The group in the meantime had come to be known as "The Artichokers"—a moniker they were not entirely happy about. Still, it stuck. The Artichokers were busily trying to interpret and propagate Tony's message. As they saw things, the ultimate meaning of Tony's speech was that the recognition of absurdity enabled a life full of meaning and connection.

Almost immediately, the Artichokers' interpretation ran into opposition from a group self-designated as "The Absurdists" (also known as "The Left Faction"), which celebrated absurdity as a way of being. The main difference between the two groups was one of emphasis. As The Absurdists saw it, The Artichokers, in their rush to achieve meaning, neglected the importance of the absurdity moment. Meanwhile The Artichokers thought The Absurdists dwelt too long in the doldrums of absurdity, unnecessarily delaying the achievement of meaning.

As many unaffiliated observers noted, this was hardly an irreconcilable difference. Still, words were exchanged. Comments posted. Some had to be taken down from the various websites, and apologies were offered. The arguments proliferated. The Absurdists held fast to the idea that the depth of meaning achieved was directly proportional to the intensity of the absurdity experienced. The Artichokers meanwhile cautioned that too much absurdity might well put meaning permanently beyond reach.

Eagle News delighted in pitting The Artichokers and The Absurdists against each other. One notorious late night show somehow managed to get two full skits out of the disputes.

Some more detached observers noted that the Artichokers and The Absurdists were coming close to re-enacting an all-too-familiar drama. This became apparent on Eagle News when one Artichoker gently chided an Absurdist by saying, "Look, we're concerned that you guys never get beyond absurdity. You never get off your own dime. You'll never get anywhere." The Absurdist representative apparently responded, "Well, you get to meaning so fast and then what do you have? You know, so you get meaning—so what? What's your encore—what's next? You're pretty much done when you get there, aren't you?" In an uncharacteristically lucid bit of insight, one of the main anchors for Eagle News summed it up: "Sounds a lot like the A-to-B thing all over again, if you ask me."

"That's right, Jack," said one of the guests. "That is *absolutely* right."

Ultimately, the Artichoker/Absurdist dispute gravitated toward a stalemate. Each side made concessions to the other but nonetheless remained true to its original insights. The Absurdists came out with their bumper sticker first: "Aburdity Happens," but the Artichokers were not far behind: "Meaning Is It."

Predictably, a third group emerged—this one known as The Authentics. They claimed that both absurdity and meaning had their place, that each depended upon the other. And—this was key to their message—it didn't really matter which one you emphasized so long as you were being authentic about it all. The Artichokers were mildly supportive. The Absurdists meanwhile had been captured by an ultra-left faction that summarily dismissed the Authentics, pointing out that authenticity didn't even take its own absurdity seriously.

And so it went. Until, as Max Stein would have put it, all the structural possibilities were exhausted. The Christian Fairfax trial (now dubbed the "sneering killer case") made a comeback on all the networks.

■ ■ ■

Among those who didn't really understand Tony's speech was John Morrison. He wouldn't have gone to Arco at all but for the fact that he lost some NCAA Final Four bet. Morrison couldn't figure out what the people in the audience wanted. And he was supremely unmoved by Tony White's heralding of absurdity.

John did appreciate some of the music and did have a fantastic date with one Sinead O'Callaghan, a red-haired Irish grad student from Boston who immediately fastened on to him and insisted they take a hike to the Arco Blue River hot springs—hot springs that did not exist. Not surprisingly, they never found the springs, but the hike did allow them to get lost in the Sawtooth Range in the midst of a brightly star-struck night. John Morrison saw his first shooting star.

John Morrison's night of wandering in the Sawtooth Range in the company of Sinead O'Callaghan did absolutely nothing, however, to bring him closer to absurdity. In fact, quite the opposite: John Morrison thought there was absolutely nothing absurd about Sinead or himself or their flash romance. It's not that he thought this new romance was reasonable or well thought out—or anything of the sort. It's just that he saw nothing absurd about it at all. Besides, as a lawyer, he tended to think of things in terms of burdens of proof, and in this regard, he was quite sure the burden of proof lay with the absurdity side of things.

Plus, it was just too hard for him to believe that the world was absurd. On the contrary, all indications suggested otherwise. Indeed, just before leaving for Arco, John Morrison had been promoted once again—this time to Tier X consultant. This promotion meant that he would oversee, integrate, and monitor Tier 1 consultants, but only when he felt the urge. The reason for this is that Tier X consultants commanded a huge hourly fee—one proportional to their prestige. It was thought that, given their extraordinary salaries, clients might balk at the cost if the Tier X consultants worked full-time. Hence, the obvious compromise: Tier X consultants dropped in on deals only whenever they felt like it. This was an arrangement John Morrison liked greatly.

Sinead too: "That's fookin' great, man. It's like a fellowship, hey love? Like, you don't really have to do anything. A fookin' MacArthur Grant for lawyers, hey?"

John Morrison couldn't recall what a MacArthur Grant was, but from Sinead's visible enthusiasm, he figured it was something really good. At any rate, being a Tier X consultant was a far cry from the drudgery of writing contingency memos back when he was just starting out. Not only was there the radically augmented salary and the work-at-your-option job description, but he also had a senior partner's corner office, which meant he could look out at the traffic on both Santa Monica Boulevard and Avenue of the Stars nearly full-time.

So life is absurd? Are you on drugs? he thought.

■ ■ ■

The big problem for David with The Event was that he had expected C to be more than just Tony. Like most everyone else, he wasn't quite sure what C would be. But he had expected something bigger. The problem with Tony's speech, for David, was that he had heard it (and agreed with it) all before. Not the speech itself, but the general ideas. He, after all, had spoken with Tony at the Berkeley conference. In fairness to Tony, David did think that his presentation was particularly clear this time. There was no talk of ontological treadmills (or ontological anythings, for that matter).

The big challenge for David was to learn something new, something as yet unseen, in Tony's speech. Driving home by way of Route 26 through the mid-latitudes of Oregon (Interstate 15 was sure to be packed), he was still trying to figure things out.

Emily was in the back seat sleeping, so David took the opportunity: "Do you think Emily got it?" he asked Eloise.

"David, she's nine!"

"Did you get anything out of it?"

Eloise thought she had understood Tony. She at least understood finally why David was so taken with Tony. But the prospect of truly accepting the absurdity of life was daunting. She sensed that Tony White's line might be a bit bleak—what some would later call nihilistic. She also perceived that it would require a complete re-evaluation of all her activities. All things considered, she wondered whether it might not be simpler to reject Tony and his ideas altogether.

David turned on the radio, and the seek function landed on a local Wyoming station. They were talking agriculture. Local agriculture.

"And so for you folks who have been caught up with all the moisture this spring, it's time to be thinking about 'rescue crops,' and I just want to say that millet is a great performer here and . . ."

Eloise tried to ignore the millet and stay focused on Tony. She looked out the window at the dying light over the desert. Tony's message frightened her a bit, but she began to explore its possibilities, the little channels of thought that it opened for her.

"And there you have it folks. We're here with Charlie Jones of Bona Fide Bird Feed & Supply talking about the possibilities of millet."

"That's right Tom and I just want to say that our bird feed makes fairly heavy use of millet, along with sunflower and sorghum. So I think there will be a market for all you people in Wyoming. And millet is just the beginning folks . . ."

David's car crested a hill and lost the Wyoming station to static. David turned down the volume. Now Eloise could focus. But what she focused on was not Tony, but millet. She knew nothing about millet. She knew nothing about Wyoming farmers and their "rescue crops." Perhaps these people were not absurd. Perhaps that was the secret to avoiding absurdity: To have *real* problems calling for *real* solutions—like looking for a good rescue crop and finding millet.

Perhaps.

She looked at David next to her and admired his profile. He had not let himself go. When she looked at him, she could still see the twenty-eight-year-old through the lines and through the sag.

Oddly, there was no comfort in that. She wondered how it had all come to this. How had she ended up with this man, in this car, driving South on I-15 back to L.A. to a disintegrating circle of friends, a Spanish stucco house she really didn't care for, and twenty-five hours of community service for misdemeanor shoplifting.

How did this happen?

She had stumbled into this life. Not blind, but not particularly attentive either. It had happened. That's what.

Against Tony, who was all about life as absurd, she thought her problem was that she hadn't taken her life seriously enough. What on earth possessed her to hook up with David?

It was the fern bar, of course. But that had all been a joke—a joke played on her by her girlfriends who said they'd meet her there and never showed. She should have known. Who in their right minds would go to a fern bar—let alone when ferns bars were one or two decades out of date?

It was supposed to be a joke, and instead she ended up married to David. Maybe it was because of the way he comforted her when they found that orange boot immobilizer thing fastened to her car. He seemed sensitive and warm. His sexual performance was barely passable. But as she thought then (and not incorrectly so), that could be fixed.

Still, it had all been so improbable. The fern bar. The drinking. The car stuff. The immobilizer. Strike just one of those things out, and she wouldn't be here next to this man, driving south on I-15 to L.A. contemplating the absurdity of her situation.

Eloise did not have the intellectual equipment or wherewithal to take these thoughts any further. Which was probably a good thing, because if she had, it would have made her predicament more dire.

She did love David—in that forty-something sense of conjugal love (a far cry from the twenty-something, over-the-top transport). But she did not love their lives together. It was—and David had used the phrase himself—too predictable.

It was as if someone or something else had made all the decisions for her and David, and they were just tagging along for the ride.

Eloise felt guilty for being so harsh. And yet it was hard to deny.

The marriage counselor hadn't helped at all. David was right: The counselor had made things worse. It was ridiculous. The counselor was ridiculous. Tier 1 was ridiculous.

"So folks unless you've already got seeds in the ground, I think millet may just be the thing for you." (David had turned the volume back on.)

"So, did you get anything out of this?" David asked.

This time Eloise mercifully did not have to answer as David's cell phone started vibrating. Bluetooth automatically channeled the sound through the car speakers.

"David, it's Mariana. Well, what did you think?"

"I thought it was fine," said David. Eloise raised her eyebrows.

"Can I interest you in a talk show circuit? I can get that for you."

"Mariana, I thought I was clear on this."

"Well, I just wanted to see if you'd changed your mind."

"Nope."

"Well, alright, but let me give you my pitch. If you—"

"No, Mariana."

"Well, if you change your mind, you know where to reach me. I'll call you next week."

David was amused by the persistence of the woman. *She just does not stop,* he thought. He wondered whether Mariana was a workaholic. And that led him to think about work generally, which in turn led to thinking about his own work. It was a concept that remained for him somewhat abstract (given that he had not actually been to the office in god knows how long). Still, he felt pretty sure he had a real occupation. Probably he was not a lawyer—given that he knew so little law. Perhaps he was a consultant of sorts—a business consultant. Maybe real estate? He hoped not.

If life was absurd, then real estate did not seem like an appropriate response.

David resolved that when he got back to L.A., he would make a truly concerted effort to work at something, somewhere. He would not go from A to B. He would resist and seek out a new job, though, of course, that would mean updating the resume and explaining that rather significant time gap when all he'd done was go from A to B. Still, now that the thing was so public and so widespread, employers would surely understand.

"Oh yes, Tom, millet is a very robust crop. Don't underestimate millet, Tom."

"Sure has been a heck of a spring, hasn't it Charlie?"

"Sure has, Tom. Sure has."

Summons

Besides Tony, perhaps the one person most disappointed with The Event was Max Stein. The truth is, Max Stein had a lot more riding on The Event than he had told anyone except Mariana.

Max Stein had helped shape Mariana's conception of The Event. A week after the Berkeley conference, Mariana heard about Max from David. The latter was evidently so impressed that Mariana contacted Max to see if he might become a client.

Max declined, but he did offer to help. At the conference, he'd had an idea. Max painstakingly explained to Mariana the cultural dissipation of meaning and the resulting breakdowns. Mariana was skeptical but nonetheless a quick study. Max suggested that the country needed an epic confrontation with absurdity—a massive cultural-artistic event where people could come together, stop their empty and mindless routines, and rebuild together more meaningful forms of life. Mariana remained dubious. But even if it didn't work, orchestrating a massive cultural event would be exactly the sort of thing that could enhance her social capital.

Again she pleaded with Max to represent him. "I could so help you with publicity, networking, branding," she said. "I could morph you into one of the three or four leading public intellectuals in the country!" Max was not sure he wanted to be morphed, and again he declined. But he did offer to help—so long as she would be willing to do a couple interviews for his book, *Meaning (and Not)*.

If Mariana's motivation was somewhat mercenary, Max Stein's was not. It was nostalgic, actually (a throwback to the '60s). Max truly did believe that a mass confrontation with the absurd in a dramatic setting ("a happening") might galvanize the creation of collective meaning—a "recovery of our alienated powers," as he put it.

Max really had believed it might work. He rested his hopes on Tony White. Max had hoped that Tony could orchestrate the confrontation and that something would come out of it. What that something would be, Max had no idea. As it turned out, neither did Tony.

The thing was doomed from the outset. What Max had wanted from Tony was simply too much to ask of a single human being. And Max ought to have known better: Nearly everything he wrote in his manuscript, *Meaning (and Not)*, should have told him that the conventional structures would win and meaning would lose.

Still, Max was not prepared for the bust that followed—the disagreements between the Artichokers and the Absurdists, the acute media coverage, and all that.

There was another thing that Max was not ready for. He was sitting at a café in Berkeley, sipping his espresso, when he opened the manila envelope that had appeared in his mailbox that morning. It was from Human Subjects (as it's called) at Berkeley. Human Subjects was the University Board of Review charged with clearing experiments by faculty on human beings. The Board's letter stated that it had received a copy of *Meaning (and Not)* and would want to see Max appear at 2:30 in the afternoon October 15 at what it ominously called "Tenure Revocation—Preliminary Hearing (Professor Max Stein)." The hearing was "preliminary," which certainly seemed like a good thing. But the hearing was on "tenure revocation," and surely that was not.

The thing is, it had never occurred to Max that The Event at Arco might qualify as the sort of human subjects research—an experiment of sorts—that would require clearance by the Human Subjects Board. And so Max had never applied.

The Hearing

"So, Dr. Stein, if I understand you correctly, you still do not think it was necessary to get clearance from Human Subjects because The Event and C and all that—they were real? And thus, according to you, not experimentation? Is that about right?"

"That is correct. I brought up the idea of a mass gathering to Mariana Fleischman, a media representative, just to push things along."

"Like when she pushed her car into Mr. Madden's Mercedes, for instance?" asked Dr. Heathland, the Chair of the Panel. He had a well-honed talent for sarcasm.

"No, Dr. Heathland. That was all her doing. Ms. Fleischman contacted me after the conference at Berkeley. That was much later."

"You became a client of Ms. Fleischman's, then?"

"No. I was never her client."

"But you worked together to shape The Event—isn't that right?"

"We did collaborate—I suggested some ideas about what The Event could look like."

"So it was a partnership essentially, then?"

"No. I simply suggested ideas."

"But you interviewed Ms. Fleischman for your book, and you made use of The Event—an event you helped shape—in your research. Isn't that correct?"

"Yes."

"And I am quoting here from page 235 of your book, *Meaning (and Not)*. Bear with me. Here it is: 'The Event was to be *an experiment* in the collective confrontation of the absurdity of human existence.' Those are your exact words—aren't they?"

"Yes."

"And we are talking about human beings here?"

"Yes."

"So what we have here, in *your own words*, is *an experiment* on human beings. Isn't that right? Never mind. I withdraw the question." Dr. Heathland's head swiveled slowly back and forth so that all present could register the disdain on his face. "I have no further questions," Dr. Heathland said, throwing down his pen on the yellow pad before him.

Another panel member started up, "Professor Stein, earlier you said this was theater you were doing. I believe that is the expression you used?"

"Yes. I said that."

"A 'happening,' you also called it—is that right?"

"Yes."

"What did you hope to accomplish? You see, I just want to make sure I understand. This hearing is ultimately about your tenure. But I want to make sure I understand just exactly what was in your mind and just how this all occurred."

"I just—" Max grasped for the right words. "I just wanted to give people the chance to reckon with the meaninglessness of their daily routines. I wanted them to recognize that they were just going from A to B. That they had fallen into this kind of absurd cultural condition that saps the meaning out of life. And ultimately I wanted to give them a chance to find meaning in their lives."

"So you were going to give them meaning? A bit presumptuous, don't you think?"

"Not at all. I wasn't trying to give them meaning. No. I wanted to offer an occasion, at most a catalyst—so that they could create their *own* meaning."

"Because *you* were sure that's what *they* needed. *You*. What did you call it earlier—you thought they should be 'awakened,' I think you said?"

"Yes."

The only member on the panel from the Board of Regents finally spoke up. "Are you a Marxist?"

"No."

"A deconstructionist, then?"

Max Stein's lawyer stood up. "If I might address the panel, I think it's getting late. My client's position may seem odd, but it is clear and, I would argue, ultimately sensible. He did not engage in any human subjects research. It was not research at all. My client was simply interacting with various persons. It's true he did, through a publicist, help prompt the idea of a public celebration of meaning in Arco, Idaho. But there was never any element of coercion. My client never invited anyone to Arco. There is simply nothing here that could be considered the kind of experimentation on human subjects that required pre-clearance. And certainly none that would warrant rescission of tenure."

The Chair looked left and looked right. "If there are no further questions . . ." The gavel came down. "We are adjourned."

It took three months for the dismissal letter to arrive at Max's home. He was asked to sign a non-disclosure agreement in exchange for which he would receive two years' worth of salary. He would lose all university privileges but retain his pension. The press took no notice. The Christian Fairfax case was now on appeal, and Christian Fairfax's lawyer had promised to reveal "stunning, *absolutely stunning*, exculpatory evidence" that would "inexorably lead to the reversal of his client's conviction."

The Wrap

As The Event receded into memory, the stories settled out—mostly, as in the way of all things cultural, by way of misunderstanding. Indeed, to say that Tony's speech in Arco was distorted would be an understatement. No American institution, it seemed—not business, not politics, not churches, not education—had any interest whatsoever in propagating the idea that human life is absurd.

They were all organized as going-enterprises with mission statements and vision statements, strategic plans and objectives. They identified critical success factors, established benchmarks, and used balanced score cards to keep track. Many of these institutions and their outputs were subject to national rankings and acted accordingly. They were all committed to enhancing human capital. They believed in branding and issued beatific slogans borrowed from TED talks. ("Be a plus, not a minus" being the most popular.) The notion, then, that these institutions (being what they were) would be helped by a recognition of the absurdity of human life was correctly perceived by nearly all of them to be a complete non-starter.

The fact that these very same institutions with all their strategic plans and benchmarks and whatnots might themselves be absurd was not something that occurred to any of them. Quite the contrary, many of them—the Catholic Bishop's conference, the Chamber of Commerce, the Republican and Democratic Parties, the Motion Picture Association of America, the ABA, the Teamsters, and the NRA issued joint statements rejecting Tony's message. Perhaps the most forceful is still available online at mylifeisnotabsurd.com.

A more studied view, first articulated by a couple of analytical philosophers, was also popularized in all the major papers:

Analytical Philosophers Discover Life Not Absurd

> *AP—Washington, D.C.* Two analytical philosophers, Dr. McCarrigan and Dr. Feeley, both of Hapton University, have recently claimed that life is not absurd. Their paper states at the outset:
>
> "The arguments supporting the absurdity of life depend upon certain non-falsifiable assumptions that lack axiological force and are not otherwise grounded in reasonableness or reasonable life plans. Moreover, not only do arguments for absurdity lack rigor, but they implicate the speaker in fatal performative contradic-

> tions. While it would not follow that life is therefore meaningful, it can be stated that the case for absurdity has been greatly overstated."

All of this opposition was, of course, a huge misinterpretation of Tony's message, which was not that life is absurd *simpliciter*, but that one had to recognize life's absurdity in order to give it meaning. This, however, turned out to be a difference that made no difference: Indeed, even if Tony's message had been correctly understood by American institutions, they would still have tried to bury it. Not the least reason was that each and every one of these institutions wanted to supply life's meaning almost always in order to get something (usually money) in exchange. Neither part—neither the meaning part nor the money part—would be possible if life turned out to be absurd. Hence, and through a logic more economic than rational, life was not absurd.

In a mildly contrarian vein, some recent Stanford graduates in the Bay Area tried to make some money by creating a web-based absurdity quotient and ranking service. Additionally, they provided answers to a multitude of questions: Which is more absurd—Cleveland or Fresno? Can absurdity cause acne? Does Belgium really have all the answers? But as with all websites on the internet (or at least most successful ones), the website at first garnered feverish interest, reached a zenith, teetered precariously on the SEO rankings, and then commenced its inexorable descent into the nether regions of the search-engine-unrecognized. Scott Daubert, newly elected president and CEO of The Future Is

Tomorrow, summed it all up on CNN: "The business of America is business, not absurdity."

The last straw came when the President of the United States declared in his State of the Union message, "The Founding Fathers created this great country so that all of us might someday be free to go from A to B. Make no mistake: Going from A to B—that is, *that has always been*, the American Dream."

Parting Shots

Max pondered the dismissal letter and the non-disclosure agreement for two days. On the second night, as he downed the last of his single malt, he decided what to do. He grabbed the lawyers' papers, set the pages aflame, and dropped them into the white kitchen sink. He was not going to keep quiet. He was going to put *Meaning (and Not)* aside and write something truly big. He would get in touch with Tony. And J.T. It was not over. Not by a long shot.

Acknowledgments

I wish to thank Elisabeth Hyde for her extraordinary graciousness in reading and commenting upon several drafts of the manuscript, Zoe Schlag for her excellent editing and editorial counseling, David Eason, Sarah Krakoff, Jack Schlegel, and Peter Shapiro for their suggestions, and Robert Hand for undertaking the project.

CPSIA information can be obtained
at www.ICGtesting.com
Printed in the USA
FFOW02n2247020516
23702FF